NOW IS THE TIME FOR RUNNING

MICHAEL WILLIAMS

LITTLE, BROWN AND COMPANY

New York   Boston

Little, Brown and Company

Hachette Book Group
1290 Avenue of the Americas, New York, NY 10104
Visit our website at www.lb-teens.com

Little, Brown and Company is a division of Hachette Book Group, Inc.
The Little, Brown name and logo are trademarks of Hachette Book Group, Inc.

The publisher is not responsible for websites (or their content) that are not owned by the publisher.

First U.S. Paperback Edition: March 2013
First U.S. Hardcover Edition: July 2011
Originally published in South Africa by Maskew Miller Longman (Pty) Ltd in 2009 as *The Billion Dollar Soccer Ball*

Library of Congress Cataloging-in-Publication Data

Williams, Michael, 1962–
[Billion dollar soccer ball]
Now is the time for running / Michael Williams. — 1st U.S. ed.
p. cm.
Summary: When soldiers attack a small village in Zimbabwe, Deo must go on the run with his older, mentally disabled brother, Innocent, carrying little but a leather soccer ball filled with money, and after facing prejudice, poverty, and tragedy, soccer gives Deo renewed hope.
ISBN 978-0-316-07790-3 (hc) / ISBN 978-0-316-07788-0 (pb)
[1. Refugees—Fiction. 2. Brothers—Fiction. 3. People with mental disabilities—Fiction. 4. Survival—Fiction. 5. Homeless persons—Fiction. 6. Soccer—Fiction. 7. Zimbabwe—Fiction.] I. Title.
PZ7.W66715Now 2011
[Fic]—dc22
                    2010043460

11

LSC-C

Printed in the United States of America

Book design by Saho Fujii

*To those who find themselves strangers
in this strange land of South Africa,
you are very welcome here.
God bless you.*

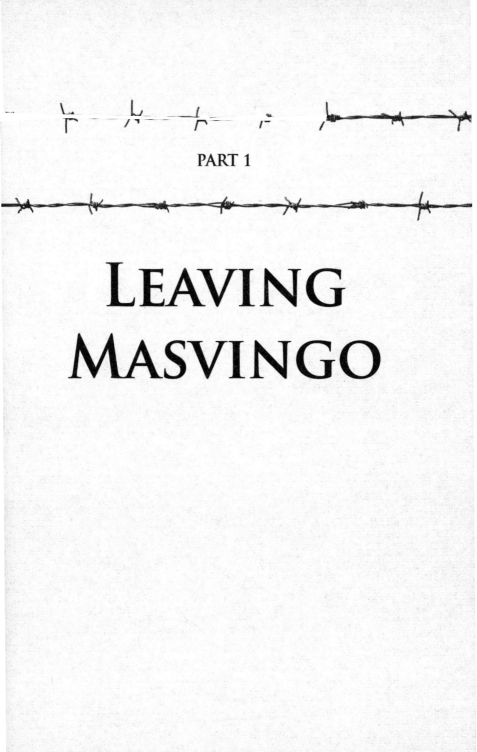

PART 1

LEAVING
MASVINGO

1

GOOOAAAL IN GUTU

The game is 2-2 when the soldiers come in their jeeps down the path to Gutu.

Javu shouts at me. "Kick, Deo, kick!"

I catch the ball between my foot and the earth and point. "The soldiers are coming," I say. The boys stop playing. They turn to look at where I'm pointing.

The president must have sent them. Perhaps he has heard how hungry we are? Grandpa Longdrop said that when there was no more *sadza*, no more cassava, and when the people cried with hunger, then the soldiers would come. He says our president will never let us go hungry. Grandpa Longdrop is never wrong, but I have never seen soldiers bringing food.

"We can still win before they get here," shouts Shadrack. "Kick, Deo. I'm open."

I turn back to the game. Javu is out right, running wide.

He has his hand up in the air, calling for the ball. If I pass to him, he will be blocked by Pelo the Buster. Javu could never get around heavy Pelo, the best defender in Masvingo Province. Better to make some Deo magic myself.

I scoop the ball up with my foot, flick it up in the air, and head it past Bhuku, who is the plodder of the group. Shadrack runs into the space to my left. This is going to be so easy.

The old one-two-three move. First touch to Shadrack, pushing the ball through the legs of Pelo, and then Shadrack sending it back onto my right foot. A quick glance up at Lola in goal, crouching now, ready to save my cannon shot — or so she thinks!

I move to kick the ball with my right foot but don't. The reason? Pelo the Buster is sliding toward me in a slow-moving heap of knobby knees, thick shins, and big feet to collect the ball and to upend me. I toe the ball into the air, jump over his legs, and kick with my left foot as hard as I can. The ball sails past Lola's open arms.

"It was too high!" she shouts. "Too high!"

"She's right, Deo. That's too high." Bhuku points at the imaginary bar my ball supposedly sailed over.

Innocent goes mad on the sidelines. He runs up and down, with his arms outstretched like the wings of an airplane, screaming, *"Goooaaal!"*

"Innocent said it's a goal," I point out. "And he can see from where he's standing."

It is always like this. When Lola misses, then the shot is always too high. I'm not sure why we let a girl play with us, but nobody else wants to be goalie, so she's useful. I like Lola and I don't like her. She can be friendly one moment and moody the next. Innocent says that's why he stays well away from girls—he can't make up his mind whether he likes them or not.

"He's your brother. Of course he thinks it's a goal." This is Bhuku again, all hands on hips, head cocked back as if he has been robbed in broad daylight.

"No use asking that one. He's crazy," says Pelo, tapping his temple with his finger. "What does he know about—"

Pelo the Buster does not have the chance to finish what he's saying because he has to deal with my fist in his mouth. Nobody talks about Innocent in front of me. Pelo should know better.

Shadrack wraps his arms around me and pulls me away. Pelo is looking to give me some of my own medicine. I glare at him, daring him to come at me, but he looks past me. Pelo the Buster can beat me any day of the week, but right now something else is more important to him than busting my brains.

The jeeps carrying the soldiers.

I hear their engines. They are closer now.

The jeeps bump and rattle down the path where only cattle and villagers coming from Mlagisa Town and Embandeni Kraal have walked. There are five, maybe six, soldiers in each jeep. Some of them are in full battle fatigues; others just wear army waistcoats and belts with ammunition. They all carry guns, porcupine quills pointing at the sky. They hold their guns as if the weapons weigh nothing. As if they are not dangerous. But I know the terrible noise they can make, and I have seen a cow cut in half from a burst of one of those guns. The soldiers look at us but don't see us.

These men have been all over Zimbabwe. They went to Zaka when the people cried with hunger, but now the people cry no more. They went to Chipinge when the people were angry from hunger, so angry that some of them were killed. Auntie Aurelia told us that her niece was one of those who were hungry. She did not say how she bled to death. Auntie Aurelia cried for seven days and then spoke about her niece no more.

The soldiers have been to faraway Kamativi, but no one speaks about what they have done there. And now they are here—in Gutu, my home.

The president said the people should not be angry. He said we were hungry because the white man was blocking the food from coming into our country. He is right about the problem of our food. We eat only enough to keep us hungry. I have heard my *amai* talk to Grandpa Longdrop about food that is supposed to come from America, but it has not come yet. My *amai* is a teacher in Gutu. She has been writing to a church in America and telling them about how we have no food here.

The truckers no longer come from South Africa. They no

longer bring stuff to fill the shelves of Mr. Singh's shop in Bikita. Grandpa Longdrop said that the road from the south is quieter than he can ever remember. Amai grows quiet, too, when he speaks of the road and its trucks. She has long since stopped going to the gas station, hoping that one special trucker might come back.

I have stopped thinking about him too. Amai doesn't talk about him anymore, and it's hard to ask questions about him. She cries or gets angry when I mention my father.

The soldiers drive past us. In the front jeep, a soldier sits with his boot up on the dashboard. He wears a red beret and sunglasses. He raises his hand, and the jeep stops with an angry spurt of dust. The soldiers standing behind him grip the crash bar. One nearly topples to the ground. The other jeeps pull up behind. Red Beret climbs out and walks toward us. His face is a mask. I notice his black belt, his revolver in a leather holster, his heavy boots, and his shiny sunglasses. I do not see his eyes but see myself twice in his glasses. I look small and bent out of shape, just a scrappy kid in blue shorts wearing a no-longer-white school shirt and standing in the dust.

"You've got a good left foot. Bring me the ball." He speaks, but I do not move. I am watching both of my scared reflections in his glasses. My mouth is open. I close it and swallow.

Pelo runs over and hands him the ball. It is no proper soccer ball. It is a pouch of cow-leather patches sewn together with twine, stuffed with tightly rolled plastic.

7

Red Beret throws my ball into the air and kicks it. The ball folds into itself. The men in the jeep laugh. He turns toward them, and they shut up. This man has broken my ball.

I am only half scared now. The other half of me is angry. He didn't need to break the soccer ball Grandpa Longdrop made for me.

"I hear there are dissidents in this village. Is that true?" His words are soft. I cannot trust them. In his question I can feel the metal teeth of a leopard trap.

I look blankly at him. If I say no, then he will know that I know what a dissident is, and then he will want to know what I know about dissidents. If I say yes, then there will be more trouble than I can even imagine.

"Who does your father vote for?"

This is a question I can answer easily. "My father does not live here. He lives on the road."

"And your father?" He looks at Pelo.

"The president," says Pelo the Buster.

The man snorts as if this was the wrong answer.

"Your game is finished."

He steps on the ball, which lets out a long fart. No one thinks it's very funny.

"I will speak to the people of Gutu and find out if what you tell me is true." The soldier is talking to all of us now. I see us in his glasses. We all look the same: small, scared children in the red dust. He turns around and walks back to the jeep.

I look around for Innocent. He is no longer standing beside

the pitch. He is scared of soldiers and must have slipped away when the jeeps arrived. I should go and look for him, but I cannot take my eyes off Red Beret.

He jumps back into the front jeep. We are forgotten now. He lifts his hand and makes a cutting gesture in the direction of our village. The driver puts his foot down, and the jeep jumps forward, causing the men at the back to grab hold of the crossbar.

As soon as the jeeps are gone, we scatter.

I throw away the rolled plastic from my dead soccer ball. The leather pouch is all I need to make a new one.

I must find Innocent. Soldiers make him nervous. And when he's nervous, he talks too much, and then there could be trouble. Blood trouble.

2

GRANDPA LONGDROP TALKS TO COMMANDER JESUS

The jeeps are parked in the center of Gutu. They are empty now. The soldiers are everywhere. I look for Innocent, but he is gone. All around me, people are moving toward Red Beret. He watches us as if we are cattle being herded across a river. His soldiers move from home to home, holding their guns in the air. Their faces show nothing. They neither smile nor shout. They neither push nor pull. But still the people move as if they are being shouted at, as if they are being pushed and pulled.

"Deo, where is your brother?" My *amai* has found me. She looks frightened.

"He ran away when the soldiers came," I say, not looking at her, knowing that she will be angry with me. Innocent may be ten years older than I am, but I always look after him. I should not have let him run away.

"You must find him, before they do. Deo! Are you listening to me? Find Innocent. You must look after your brother."

Amai is worried, looking around but not seeing her special son.

But it's too late. One of the soldiers walks up to us. I cannot slip away. Behind him, I see Grandpa Longdrop coming out of our home. My *amai* calls to him, and the soldier allows her to fetch him. I feel better now that Grandpa Longdrop is here.

Grandpa Longdrop puts his arm around my shoulders and leads me to where everyone else has gathered. His hand may be wrinkled, but it is strong. His face may look like the cracked, dried mud of the water hole, but his eyes are always kind.

"Have you seen Innocent?" I whisper to him.

He shakes his head and lifts his finger to his lips. Perhaps he has hidden Innocent. I've learned to expect the unexpected from Grandpa Longdrop. He knows so much about everything that sometimes his words make me dizzy. He can tell you about the planets. When it will rain and when it won't, when to plant beans and when to watch for the calves to drop. How electricity works and where the dead go when they die.

Of course he would kill me if he knew I called him Grandpa Longdrop. But the story of how he was born made me laugh so hard that I always think of him as Grandpa Longdrop. Amai told me how her grandmother gave birth to her son while she was sitting on the long-drop. She pushed too hard going to the toilet and if it weren't for the umbilical cord, they would have had to fish the newborn baby out of the shit. Your grandfather is a survivor, she said to me. He survived his birth, the liberation war, running the white man's farm, and now old age — he can survive anything. His real name is Grandpa Doro.

We face Red Beret, who waits for us to be silent. Lola and her family are brought forward. She has two older brothers, who look scared. The soldiers hold them by their arms. Perhaps they were trying to run away?

We wait for Red Beret to speak.

"Bring me the food."

This is not what I expected. Does he not know we have nothing, that there is no food here? I see the adults look at one another as if he has asked them for diamonds, or gold bars, or television sets.

Food? Why would he want what we do not have?

"Bring. Me. The. Food." One of the soldiers repeats Red Beret's command. His words sound like the hiss from a snake.

All around me, the adults talk at once to one another. The men send the women back to their homes. My *amai* looks at Grandpa Longdrop with a question in her eyes, and he nods to her an answer I do not understand.

"Amai?"

She waits for Grandpa Longdrop to tell her to go. She is the last of the women to go to her home. I look up at Grandpa Longdrop, and he squeezes my shoulder.

"We need to listen to these men, Deo. These are our president's men. He has sent them here with good reason."

Grandpa Longdrop loves the president. He fought with him in the war for liberation. He's told me stories about how he met the president when he was a younger man, how they fought together in the bush, how the president promised them freedom, and how they won the war against the colonizers. Because he was loyal to the president, he was given a farm. It was good for a while, living on that farm. I don't know why we had to leave. Grandpa Longdrop doesn't talk about the farm much. But he loves the president and is a proud member of Zed, the president's political party.

The women return with pots of porridge, a few ears of corn, plates of offal, pumpkin leaves, okra, black pap scraped from the bottom of the pot, a basket of eggs, chickens tied up at the ends of poles. The pile grows in front of Red Beret, but he does not look at it. If this is all the food in Gutu, a village of more than a hundred people, it is not very much. Looking at what our neighbor has, I see that he has no more than we do. Pelo's *amai* has brought her goat. It is skinny and bleats to be let free.

Amai brings our food. Red Beret watches her as she places it in front of him. He smiles at my *amai* with the grin of a hyena.

Grandpa Longdrop feels my muscles tense. He squeezes my shoulder in warning.

"This is not the food I am looking for." Red Beret speaks

again and pulls a paper from his pocket. "Who is the teacher in Gutu?"

I feel my *amai* stiffen beside me. She steps forward.

Red Beret holds out the paper and calls her with the finger of his right hand. She walks forward, takes the paper from him, and reads it. My *amai* is braver than I've ever seen her. She stands with her shoulders straight. He is taller, much taller, but she holds his gaze.

"It has not arrived yet," she says.

He nods. "When will it come?"

"Any day. Maybe tomorrow. Maybe the next."

He nods again, sends her back to us.

"Amai, what's going on?" There is something she is not telling me. She glares at me with that if-you-speak-one-more-word-you'll-feel-my-wooden-spoon look, so I shut up.

A few of the soldiers move forward to collect the food and start loading it into the jeeps. We look on like dumb animals as the food is taken away from us. What is going on? I want to scream, This is all we have. Why are you taking away our food?

Red Beret speaks.

"I am Commander Jesus. I am one of the president's men. I was once a leader of Five Brigade. The president has sent me here because he is unhappy with how you voted in the election. Most of you know that this country was won by the barrel of the gun. There are some among you who fought in the war of liberation. I see it in your eyes. You know who you are, and you should be ashamed of your neighbors. You know what sacrifices were made for the freedom we now enjoy. Should we now let it go at the stroke of a pen? Should one just write an X and let the country go just like that? You voted wrongly at the election. You were not thinking straight. That is why the president sent me here.

"In the back of my jeep there is a drum filled with blood. The blood came from people who voted wrongly. My life is to drink human blood. My supply is running low. I have come here to kill dissidents and not to play with them.

"You are going to eat eggs, after eggs hens, after hens goats, after goats cattle. Then you shall eat cats, dogs, and donkeys. Then you are going to eat your children. After that you shall eat your wives. Then the men will remain, and because dissidents have guns, they will kill the men and only dissidents will remain. That's how we will find who they are, and then we will kill them."

The groaning starts behind me from some of the older women. Some of the people begin crying. Pelo's *amai* grabs her head and wails as if she has been burned. Lola's brothers whimper. The ha-ha birds rise from the trees and screech away across the sky.

In my nose I smell something terrible. It is worse than burnt sour milk, worse than dog crap, worse than a day-old dead rat.

It is the smell of fear.

I stare at the jeeps. I can see no drums. What is Commander

Jesus talking about? Grandpa raises his hand and steps out of the group. My stomach somersaults.

"May I speak to Commander Jesus?" he asks in a voice that stills the groaning women.

Commander Jesus nods and watches Grandpa Longdrop with interest.

"My name is Dixon Nyandoro, once Sergeant Nyandoro, veteran of the struggle for liberation and supporter of the president. I fought to free this country from the white oppressor and did not rest until such time as the snake's head had been cut off. I was given a farm when we took back the land from the white man, and I have been a loyal supporter of Zed all my life. There are no dissidents in Gutu. I know of no one here who would betray our president, and—"

"You know of this?" Commander Jesus flaps the paper he showed Amai in Grandpa Longdrop's face. "You know that there are people starving while you accept food from foreigners who will steal this election? Are you an imperialist? Do you support the puppet of the West?"

"My daughter runs a school that is supported by a church in America." Grandpa Longdrop's voice trembles. It is hard to tell if he is angry or afraid. "This church has sent some food because we have nothing here...."

"Nothing! That is a lie. See the food that my men have collected. Masvingo Province was lost in the election to the oppressors' puppet. Your village's votes were counted, and we know that many of you voted wrongly. Now lie down!"

Commander Jesus raises his hand. The soldiers lower their guns toward us.

A great wail of agony fills the air. We know what is coming and can do nothing to stop it now.

"On the ground," the soldiers scream. "Lie down! Lie down!"

My cheek hits the ground, but Grandpa Longdrop remains standing. "But you cannot do this to us. The president would not allow you to—"

"I said lie down!"

I hear an awful crunch and see Grandpa Longdrop collapse in front of me. His eyes look dazed. He tries to get up, and I try to reach him to tell him to stay down, but then Commander Jesus kicks him. He crumples. The sense goes out of his eyes. Someone is screaming. At the moment when I realize who is screaming, I see him.

Innocent.

Innocent runs screaming toward Commander Jesus with a stick raised high above his head. He cracks it down on Commander Jesus's outstretched hands.

"No! Innocent, don't!"

It is too late. The soldiers are on him.

3

BEATING INNOCENT

The soldiers beat Innocent with their rifle butts.

What is worse than the sound of wood against the bones of your brother? I cannot think of anything worse than that.

Innocent does not cry. He lies like a baby, curled up, his hands and arms covering his head.

Commander Jesus holds his injured hand. I wish it broken, but then unwish it. If his hand is broken, he might kill Innocent.

Amai cries for them to stop. She runs toward Commander Jesus, but he pushes her away. Grandpa Longdrop is still on the ground. Tears roll down my face.

My brother is dying before my eyes. And it is my fault. I should never have let him run away. I should have kept him close to me at all times. I should have brought him home from the soccer game. I should have held his hand when we were gathered before Commander Jesus. I want to run to Commander Jesus and throw myself at his feet and beg him to stop the soldiers, but my *amai* has both her arms around me.

Finally, Commander Jesus stops the soldiers.

Innocent is pulled to his knees. His face is crooked, his eyes black balls. Blood trickles from his broken nose.

"When you strike Commander Jesus, you strike our president," Commander Jesus says softly. "How many here would like the opportunity of striking me?"

Cries of fear come from the people of Gutu. They know what will follow. Some of the soldiers have taken long sticks from the jeeps. The others stand with their rifles lowered, pointing at us. There is nothing we can do.

The soldiers beat us as we lie on the ground.

At least they have stopped beating Innocent. They have thrown him at the feet of Commander Jesus.

Useless hands against hard sticks. Elbows cracked. Heads smacked.

Screams.

Flashes of wood. Soldiers grunting.

And pain. Lots of it.

4

OPERATION WHO DID YOU
VOTE FOR

Grandpa Longdrop says that there are two kinds of people, those who believe in the Spirits and those who don't. I think I am one of the first kind of people, but I can't be sure. I understand the Spirits of the Wind, the Spirits of the Rocks, and the Spirits of the Trees are all those who have died and live on in other ways. I understand that they watch over us, that they can sometimes be angry because we forget them. And it is said that when they are angry, they can sometimes punish us.

But this thing of the beating is too big to blame on the Spirits. They would not allow such a painful thing to happen. If I believe in Spirits, why would I believe in something that causes such pain? Surely the Spirits had nothing to do with what has happened in our village.

I can think only that there must be some mistake. Perhaps our neighbors did vote wrongly. Perhaps they put their X next to the wrong name. Perhaps everyone is lying to everyone else. I cannot always tell when adults are telling the truth.

Like now, when I ask my *amai* what will happen to us, all she says is: "It will be all right, Deo. It will be all right."

I don't believe her. I don't think she believes her own words.

We sit huddled together on the ground and wait for I don't know what. We have been sitting here for a night and a whole day. Grandpa Longdrop lies on the ground, his head in my *amai*'s lap. Sometimes he groans, and sometimes he is so quiet that I am afraid that he will never wake up.

The soldiers have taken my brother away. They dragged him into the bush beyond the village. I don't know what they have done to him. If they knew Innocent, they would never hurt him.

The backs of my legs hurt where the soldiers' sticks fell, but this is nothing to what others have suffered. One of Lola's brothers has a broken arm. Bhuku's *amai* has a split in her head that bleeds and bleeds. Shadrack's little sister could be dead.

The small children cry; they are thirsty. I am thirsty too, but I will not cry. The women beg for water, but the soldiers are suddenly deaf. Commander Jesus says that he is waiting for the food from the American church.

My *amai* is hurt too, but she is hurt more inside. Late last night the soldiers came and took her away to have a long talk with Commander Jesus in one of the huts. I waited for her, but she must have come back when I was asleep. I dreamed my *amai* was crying so hard that her tears filled a river. When I woke up I realized it wasn't a dream — she was crying, but silently. She would not speak when I asked her what Commander Jesus wanted to talk to her about. She just shook her head in a way that made my heart hurt.

She is worried sick about Innocent. She does not care for herself. How can any of this be all right? I wonder to myself. But I don't speak it out loud.

In the afternoon, when the heat has made my tongue thick in my mouth, the truck arrives. The soldiers run to their jeeps and drive out to meet the truck. I see some people run away into the bushes. Others are too scared to run.

Grandpa Longdrop does not move. My *amai* lays his head down and watches as the truck driver is pulled from the cab. One of the soldiers kicks him and he runs away. I don't see him again.

Commander Jesus walks over to the truck and opens the flaps of the back. Inside there are wooden boxes with writing on them. PINTO BEANS. CANNED FRUIT. POWDERED MILK. MAIZE. The soldiers seem very happy now. They have lost their masks. They seem like boys now. Even Commander Jesus is smiling. He calls for the men to take some of the boxes of food down from the truck.

"Perhaps they will give us some?" It is Pelo the Buster.

"Maybe they will let us go now," says Bhuku.

I have no time for this stupid talk. The stars will fall from the sky before the soldiers give us food.

I must find Innocent.

While everyone is watching the soldiers, while the soldiers and Commander Jesus are looking at the boxes in the back of the truck, I slip away. I run to our home. Inside, everything is a mess. There is no sign of Innocent.

I go to the far end of the village and look behind every hut, whispering Innocent's name. I run faster now because it won't be long before Commander Jesus will notice that some of the people have left. I go to the old thorn *kraal* where we used to keep our cattle.

A naked body is lying in the middle of the *kraal*. The man's wrists are tied to pegs in the ground. His ankles are tied to the end of a log that stretches his legs wide apart.

There is a sack over his head.

The man doesn't move. I think he must be dead.

"Innocent?" I kneel down beside the body, not wanting it to be my brother. I notice ants crawling all over his body.

I try to take off the sack. It is wet. The cords of the sack have been tied around his neck. I struggle to untie the knots. It can't be my brother.

My brother's eyes flicker open. He stares up at me.

He is not dead.

His smile makes him look like a monster. There is dried blood at the side of his mouth, his nose is broken, and his eyes are all puffy.

"No, don't move...."

"Deo..."

I am crying when I hear my name. Innocent is alive.

"I need to get these out of the ground," I say, wiping my tears from my eyes, and then I begin to pull up the pegs. They pop out of the ground. I untie the wire wrapped around his ankles and the log and help him to stand up.

"Deo, I am sorry I am dirty. They peed on me."

His head is trembling. Innocent hates to be dirty. He washes his hands twenty or thirty times a day. He goes through soap like children go through sweets. He washes his clothes so often that Amai is always complaining that she has to buy him new ones. I think he might be having one of his fits. Amai always knows what to do when Innocent has a fit. She rolls him on his side and tries to stop him from swallowing his tongue. I don't think I can do that. Not now.

"Not now, Innocent, please not now," I say. "We'll have a wash together. I promise you soap and hot water. Just the way you like it. Promise."

"I need to wash," he says, looking in disgust at his arms and legs and brushing off the ants that crawl over him.

"I've got to get you away from the soldiers. Try to walk."

"Deo, the soldiers took my clothes. I need my pants." He speaks softly, covering himself with his hands. Innocent is shy about being naked. Even when Amai helps him dress, she must always turn around when he puts on his underpants.

"I'll get you some more clothes," I say quietly, trying to keep fear out of my voice. He hates being rushed, and I must force myself to speak slowly, as if we are in no great hurry.

"We must go now. We don't want the soldiers to come back and take my clothes too. Then we'll both be naked. That will be terrible. The two Doro brothers running around like naked monkeys. Can you imagine everyone laughing at our butts and our balls bouncing around?"

He understands that. He nods his head up and down, up and down, until it starts trembling again.

"Doro brothers naked as monkeys. Not very funny, Deo," he says seriously, worried about people seeing him without his clothes. "Nobody must see our butts. That's just plain rude."

This idea gets him walking. I half carry, half drag him to the other side of the *kraal*. I'll need to hide him until I can get him away. There are some pipes down by the river. A long time ago they were meant to get water to Gutu, but nothing came of the Gutu Water Project. One day a big truck brought the pipes, unloaded them by the river, and then drove away and never came back. No one ever fetched the pipes, and they have been here forever. When I was smaller, we played in them. Now they will be a perfect place to hide Innocent.

But every minute I am away from the village is danger for my *amai* and Grandpa Longdrop. We hurry. Innocent limps, then runs a bit, then stumbles. I struggle to keep him up. Soon we are at the pipes. I choose one closer to the dry riverbed, far from the village.

"Get in here," I say.

Innocent ducks his head and crawls in. I follow behind and

make sure he lies down. I collect some dried bushes and block the entrance to the pipe. The hiding place is not perfect, but it is all I can think of.

"Don't come out of here. Okay, Innocent? Don't come out."

He nods. "They mustn't hurt him. I couldn't let them hurt Grandpa Longdrop."

"He'll be fine. Grandpa Longdrop will be all right," I say, knowing that I sound like my *amai*. Knowing that I am lying to him the same way adults can lie.

I must get back to the village.

I run along the dry riverbed and head up the small slope to the village. I don't want to go back. But what if Commander Jesus is looking for me? What if he hurts my *amai* because I ran away?

Gunshots *rat-a-tat-tat* across the valley.

The noise makes me stumble. My ears are deaf for a bit but come to life when the gunshots *rat-a-tat-tat* again. I get up and start running, fear chasing me every step of the way.

5

BLOOD FOR DRUMS

I crawl forward into the noise of people dying.

The soldiers are shooting. People are running away. Some are falling. Now the soldiers hold their guns as if they mean business. Their guns bark, come alive in their hands, their bullets rip into the earth, the walls, trees, pots, chairs, and flesh.

I watch. I am too afraid to turn away.

People scream; their cries are cut in half by bullets.

In the noise and panic, I cannot see Amai. I cannot see Grandpa Longdrop.

At last the shooting and screaming stops. My ears ring with dreadful silence. I slowly get up onto my knees, but no one sees me.

The soldiers climb into their jeeps and drive up the path out of Gutu. Behind them the truck with food follows.

I wait until they are gone, until the jeeps are out of sight. Then I run into a place that is no longer my home. I stand in a village that is no longer the place where I live. There is nothing left of that place. There is nothing left of our neighbors. Nothing left of babies playing in doorways. Nothing left of fires cooking food. Nothing left of the smiles and greetings of people who know you. Nothing left of Grandpa Longdrop's stories. Nothing left of the touch of my *amai*.

I find her in the dust.

Amai is lying facedown. Her arms are thrown out in front of her as if she is trying to grab something out of her reach. Her back is covered with a damp patch of blood. I carefully turn her over, lift her head.

She does not call my name. She does not look at me. She will never call my name again; she will never see me again.

Amai is dead.

I find Grandpa Longdrop. He stares up at the sky. His mouth is open. He does not look like Grandpa Longdrop anymore.

I find Shadrack. Dead.

There is Lola. Blood where her face should be. Her brothers are lying not far away.

Everything is so still after the gunshots. It is as if all the sound has been sucked out of the air. My ears are humming with the dullness after a great noise, and it's hard to breathe.

I feel a burning lump in my chest. It rises in me. It will make me fall to the ground and cry and cry and cry. I can't let it come up to my throat. I push it down. Pinch my cheeks hard. So hard it makes my eyes water. The burning lump smolders in my stomach.

I must get Innocent away from here. He cannot see what I have seen.

He cannot see Amai lying in the dust.

At home, I scratch around for his clothes and grab whatever I can carry. The soldiers will come back. They will come looking for us. They will shoot again. Commander Jesus will drink more blood. He will come back to fill the drum in the back of his jeep. He is not happy until he has drunk all the blood of all the dissidents. Somebody must have lied in this village. The president would not do this if people had voted correctly. Grandpa Longdrop would still be alive if people had voted properly. My *amai* too.

I run back to the pipes, carrying Innocent's clothes. He is still in the pipe, behind the bushes. I find him shivering, curled up, and holding himself. He looks at me as if I am a ghost.

"I heard the guns, Deo. I was scared. Why do they make so much noise?"

"Here are your clothes." I hand them over, and he holds them in front of him.

"Turn around," he says.

"Innocent..."

"Turn around!"

I turn around while he dresses.

"Grandpa Longdrop and Amai have been taken by the soldiers to meet the president." I don't know why I say this, but the words jump out of my mouth. "Commander Jesus has taken them to explain what has happened in Gutu. He is very sorry for what the soldiers did to you and wants Grandpa Longdrop and Amai to explain their actions too."

"The president will understand," says Innocent.

"But we have to leave Gutu. Grandpa Longdrop said that there are lots of bad soldiers who do not support the president. They will kill us if they find us. They will take away our clothes and hurt us. So we must leave."

"Okay, you can turn around now, Deo."

"We have to leave. The bad soldiers might come back."

Innocent nods slowly. "But my Bix-box, Deo? My Bix-box."

I had forgotten about Innocent's Bix-box. Years ago, Amai went into Harare with Innocent and bought a two-for-one packet of Weet-Bix cereal. The shop gave a rectangular tin box with the two packets of Weet-Bix — for free. Innocent thought it was Christmas when Amai gave the box to him. From that day onward, his Bix-box was all that mattered. He put everything he loved in his Bix-box, the main treasure being his precious radio. Nobody was allowed to see what he kept inside, and he buried it in a place that he thought no one knew. We all pretended we had no clue where he hid his treasure, but living in one room makes it hard to hide anything.

"I'll get you another Bix-box...." I know this is the wrong thing to say, but I am desperate to leave.

Innocent's eyes darken, and his jaw sticks out. He won't go

anywhere without his Bix-box. He dips his head onto his chest and shakes it from side to side.

"No, no, no, no!" He says each *no* louder and louder.

I should have remembered his stupid box when I was getting his clothes, but my head was filled with Amai in the dust and the strange shape of Grandpa Longdrop's open mouth.

"You know, sometimes you can be a pain in the butt, Innocent!"

Innocent nods his head up and down, not looking at me. He knows he will win this argument.

"It's not my fault I'm a pain in your butt, Deo," he says, nodding. "It's not my fault. You know that, Deo. It's the doctor's fault. It's not my fault."

"Okay, okay, you can stop with the sorry-for-Innocent act. Promise me you'll stay here."

I leave him nodding his head.

"And soap, Deo. Innocent is dirty," he calls after me. "Look at my hands. It's not good to be dirty. Amai says the Germans will make you sick."

He means germs.

I pile the bushes in front of the pipe again. Smoke curls from one of the huts in the village. It seems very still. Too still. I don't want to walk among the dead again, but I have no choice.

In the village the air smells of burning wood, blood, and machine oil. I do not look at the bodies. I walk quickly to our hut.

Innocent always buries his Bix-box at the back of the hut in a hole. I lift the flat rock and find his box. My hands are shaking, and I keep hearing noises. Perhaps the soldiers are back? I must get out of here. I grab the leather pouch Grandpa Longdrop made for me. It doesn't seem possible that I will ever play soccer again, but I pick up the pouch anyway.

I know where Amai hides our money. When I open the side of the mattress, I see that somebody has come before me. The money is gone. I go to her second hiding place, inside her pillow. I find several fifty million dollar notes, a few more hundred million dollars. There is no time to count it all. It's not much, but it will buy us some food. The only problem is how to carry all the notes.

I stuff them into the leather pouch. The money fills out the ball nicely, and I find a piece of string and sew up the patch. I toss the ball into the air. Nobody will know I have a billion dollars in my soccer ball.

Outside, I give one last look at Amai. I wish she would rise from the dust, wipe her hands on her apron, and smile at me again. I wish she would call me in for food and tell me sternly not to forget my homework. I want to kneel beside her and cry, but Innocent is waiting for me and the soldiers might come back.

I go and stand before Grandpa Longdrop. He seems smaller than I remember. "Thank you for the soccer ball, Grandpa Longdrop. I'll always keep it with me," I say and wonder if he hears me wherever he is.

There is nothing left for me here.

When I get back to the pipes, Innocent is waiting for me. I hand him his Bix-box.

"You didn't look inside?" he asks.

"No, of course not. Come on, let's go."

Innocent takes out his small radio and turns it on. He starts searching for a station. His thumb moves expertly on the dial.

I know what he is looking for. "There are no soccer games today, Innocent."

"I'm just looking," he says, turning the sound down and looking at me as if I have just told him he's stupid. He holds the small radio close to his ear, and I don't have to worry about him anymore until he is hungry. Once Innocent gets into radio land he's in another world. He walks a bit stiffly, painfully.

I never know what Innocent does with pain. Ever since I can remember he hasn't felt pain like the rest of us do. Amai said it has something to do with his nerves and the messages they send to his brain. She said the messages are a bit slow. Sometimes his brain doesn't register the pain until long after it is over. Innocent was badly hurt by the soldiers. He flinches when he walks, but he doesn't complain. He is lost in radio land.

We walk away from Gutu without looking back. I wonder whether I will ever see this place again. I hope not. Gutu is the place where Amai and Grandpa Longdrop died. This is no longer a place where people live.

This is a place where my people died.

6

CAPTAIN WASHINGTON IN BIKITA

We walk to Bikita to see Captain Washington. He is the best policeman in the district. I will tell him what happened to us in Gutu, what happened to Amai and Grandpa Longdrop and the others. He will know what to do. Bikita is three hours' walk on the normal path from Gutu, but we do not walk on that path. It is the road that the soldiers used. If they should come back they will see us. We walk the long way.

After two hours of walking I hear the batteries slowly dying in Innocent's radio. This is another sort of trouble with Innocent. Battery trouble. He hates it when his radio dies and there are no fresh batteries to keep it alive. Amai always kept a supply of batteries on the top shelf of our hut for these emergencies. If Innocent can't turn his radio on, he goes crazy. I mean really crazy. Screaming and breaking things and swearing so bad it makes your toes curl. I'm a little scared of my big brother when he gets like that. Grandpa Longdrop says it's when the curtain is lifted in Innocent's brain and we can see how much damage was done when he was born. He said it is a reminder to us of how well Innocent does to keep everything under control most of the time. Grandpa Longdrop said that the Spirits had gone to sleep when Innocent was born. Amai always rolled her eyes when Grandpa spoke of Innocent's birth. She said it was the doctor who was asleep and didn't get Innocent out of her in time.

And I forgot the batteries. So stupid! He turns the dial up, presses the radio close to his ear, and shoots me a worried glance. He will be coming out of radio land soon, and I'd better find something to keep him from worrying about his silent radio.

Innocent is like that. There always has to be one thing he is busy with. He must be washing his hands, eating, listening to his radio, helping Grandpa Longdrop sweep the yard, or taking the garbage to the dump for Amai.

We approach a baobab tree. It's time for a fruit break.

"Turn off the radio, Innocent. Let's eat."

I climb up the great branches of the baobab tree and pick the huge fruit. I drop them down to Innocent. Soon we have a pile at the foot of the tree. I break open the hard shell and pull out the soft fruit inside, handing some to my brother. We eat in silence, juice running down the sides of our mouths.

"Where are we going, Deo?"

I have no answer. Captain Washington, I could say, but then where?

"Deo?"

I am eating and thinking. This is a problem that needs lots of thinking. My *amai* has a sister in Harare, but the road to Harare is very long and filled with soldiers and roadblocks. My aunt is uneasy around Innocent. I don't want to arrive there and tell her the bad news from Gutu.

I am thinking now and not eating.

"Here. Look." Innocent hands me a photograph that he has taken from his Bix-box.

It is a color picture of a man standing with his right arm around Amai. She is smiling. The man is hugging Innocent with his left arm. Innocent is grinning as if he has just been tickled. He is a lot younger. I was not yet born when this photo was taken. Behind them is a great big truck with the word REMOVALS written on its side.

"Mr. Goniwe," says Innocent. "Mr. Goniwe lives in Good-wood." He shows me the words on the side of the truck with his knuckles, his fingers pointing to the ground.

"It's in South Africa, Innocent. We can never get there," I say, wiping my mouth with the back of my hand. I have never seen this photo. Mr. Goniwe is my father too. My mother has shown me some others, but not this one. I am angry for no reason I can think of. I look at the man embracing Innocent. There is no photo of me this close to my father.

"Goodwood must be a good place." Innocent puts the photograph back into his Bix-box, and the conversation about our father is over, because I see people coming along the same way we have come.

We hide in the bushes. You can't trust anybody these days. They are not from Gutu. The men carry suitcases; the women carry their small children on their backs and parcels on their heads. They pass a little way in front of us. They do not look happy. They walk as if they carry rocks, and they look scared. Perhaps they have some kind of sickness. Some of the men have bandages around their heads; one of them is helping a boy my age, struggling on crutches. I see that he has only one leg. Bikita is still another hour away. It must be hard to walk with only one leg. Perhaps they took this path because they are also afraid of the soldiers?

"I am glad the soldiers didn't take my leg," whispers Innocent.

We wait for them to pass, and then we go. We must get to Captain Washington's house before it gets dark. Perhaps there is an English Premier League game on his television. Captain Washington has a satellite dish, and he allows us to watch soccer whenever we come to Bikita. I think Captain Washington is kind to us because he has no wife and no children. Amai always made sure that when we visited him she brought food and the foreign magazines she gets as a schoolteacher. I think Captain Washington is soft on Amai. She said he was becoming as big as a hippo with all the food she was making for him. Captain Washington always laughed at my *amai*'s jokes. She can make you feel like you're the only person in the world that's important. She's like that.

She *was* like that.

The burning lump in my chest rises into my throat. I swallow it down. My eyes water again, but I will not cry. Sadness makes me walk faster.

Innocent's radio is softer. He pushes it hard against his ear. I know he can't hear very much. He'll get desperate pretty soon.

We get to Bikita just before battery trouble.

"My radio's dying, Deo."

"You'd better hide it," I say.

Innocent looks as if he is going to explode. He pushes it into my hands, wanting me to fix it, wanting me to make it right.

"Put it away before the soldiers see it. We'll go to Mr. Singh's shop."

The shadows are long. There is something strangely different in the air. It is nothing like normal, sleepy Bikita. The people run from place to place. The doors are shut. Curtains are drawn. There is no one sitting on the steps by the office building. But before I do anything, I must get batteries for Innocent. He looks like he will burst. He sways from one foot to the other and slaps the side of his head as if mosquitoes are biting him.

Innocent and I go into the Bread and Milk Shop. Mr. Singh is looking out the window nervously.

"Can I have some batteries? Four radio batteries."

He doesn't greet us but goes to the shelf behind the counter and gets the batteries. I don't know why it is called the Bread and Milk Shop. There is never any milk or bread here. The shelves look emptier than last time I was here, but thank goodness Mr. Singh has batteries. He doesn't recognize me without Amai or Grandpa Longdrop. Usually he smiles at me, asks me how school is. Now he seems busy with something else that makes him look as if he's got ants running up and down his legs. While he gets the batteries, I take some money out of the soccer ball.

I give him the money, but he shakes his head.

"They cost three times that amount now," he says.

I'm confused. "But why, Mr. Singh?"

"Inflation."

I don't understand but give him more money to pay for the inflation anyway. I don't think Mr. Singh would cheat me, but how can something cost three times more in a month's time?

Mr. Singh is looking out the window again.

"What's happening?" I ask.

"Operation Who Did You Vote For," he says. He looks worried. Very worried. "They are calling for a *pungwe* tonight."

"What's a *pungwe*?"

"A time for Zed to remind us why we are lucky to have our president," says Mr. Singh. "They call it Operation Rehabilitation."

I want to ask him more questions, but he shoos me out of the shop and locks the door behind me. I hand Innocent his batteries, and he grins like a toothpaste ad. He hands me the radio.

"Make the radio work again, Deo."

"I'll put them in later. Now we must get to Captain Washington."

We run through the streets to the policeman's house at the end of town. When we arrive, Captain Washington is standing on a ladder working on his satellite dish. "Hey, Captain Washington! What are you doing?" I shout, and he drops his screwdriver in fright.

"Deo! What are you doing here?" He climbs down the ladder and smiles nervously at Innocent and me. He must have been sleeping in his uniform. It is all crumpled and dirty. He seems surprised to see us, almost embarrassed.

"Innocent? What happened to your face?"

Innocent ducks his head, raises his hands to hide his face.

"What are you doing?" I ask, pointing at the dish that is hanging half off the wall. I don't want to tell him what happened in Gutu. Not yet.

"I have to take down the dish. It's Operation Pull Down the Satellite Dish."

Innocent finds this very funny. He starts giggling, his hand in front of his mouth, and his whole body starts shaking.

"And you, Innocent, why are you laughing?"

"Operation Go to the Toilet, please," he says, pointing to the house.

Captain Washington can't help but smile at my brother.

"Operation Open the Door," says Innocent, standing in front of the closed door. I roll my eyes at Captain Washington. This will be the Big Joke for at least the next two weeks.

Captain Washington has a large house made of bricks. It has a kitchen, a bedroom, and the best thing of all, a bathroom with a flush toilet and a shower. But the main thing about his house is the lounge where the television stands in one corner. Innocent and I have sat here many times watching English Premier soccer matches. Manchester United against Chelsea. The best games, though, are the Africa Cup games. Senegal against Nigeria in last year's Africa Cup finals. This room is why I liked coming to Bikita with Amai. Innocent and I would sit here staring at the television while Amai and Captain Washington would talk in his bedroom. It is in Captain Washington's lounge that I have met all the giants of soccer: Drogba, Ronaldinho, David Beckham. I know all their names, what goals they scored, what positions they play.

I liked our visits to Captain Washington for another reason — they always made my *amai* happy. I think she's soft on the captain too. She would join Innocent and me when she had finished talking with Captain Washington in his bedroom. She was always smiling a secret smile as if he had told her the funniest joke on Earth. And the captain always

looked pleased after he had spent some private time with
Amai.

Innocent goes straight for the toilet. He will spend the next
twenty minutes washing his hands, long enough for me to
tell Captain Washington what happened to us.

"Where is your mother?" he asks once he has closed the
front door.

And so I tell him.

Everything there is to be told.

It is not good to see adults cry. They should not cry in front
of children. Captain Washington sobs. I don't know where
to look or what to say. I hold my billion-dollar soccer ball in
my lap and wait for Captain Washington to stop crying. He
holds his face in his hands, and his shoulders shake. I pick at
the twine holding the soccer ball together.

I would love to get a new soccer ball. I wonder how much
they cost.

I wish he would stop.

I tell him that Innocent does not know about Amai and
Grandpa Longdrop. I ask him not to tell my brother.

He nods, wipes his eyes and the snot from his nose. He gets
up and goes to the kitchen. He brings back a bottle of booze.
He pours himself a drink and swallows it quickly. I haven't
seen Captain Washington like this. Normally he is very neat.
His uniform is always pressed, his hat always clean. At least
when he drinks, he is no longer crying.

Innocent comes into the room. "Operation Clean Up

Innocent," he says, showing us his hands, washed pink-clean. He does look better, even happy. The swelling on his face is still bad, but his eyes shine, and I think he has forgotten what happened in Gutu. He always feels comfortable here — this is like a second home to him.

"Innocent is hungry, Captain. Operation Feed Innocent?" This is my brother trying his luck, smiling in the way only Innocent can smile. He is not shy among people he knows.

I must admit I am pretty hungry myself, but I don't say anything. Sometimes it's handy having Innocent around. I'm pleased when Captain Washington goes into the kitchen and pulls out some food from the fridge and puts it on the table. We stand around in the kitchen and eat okra and pumpkin leaves and my absolute favorite food in the whole world — leftover duck.

"Your mother always made the best duck," he says, cutting us pieces of the white meat with brown skin. "I loved it when she cooked for me. Your mother was such a good woman, Innocent." Captain Washington heats some water on the Primus stove for some tea. I wish he wouldn't talk about Amai in the past tense in front of Innocent.

I am halfway through my cup of tea when there is loud banging on the door. Captain Washington flashes me a warning look.

"Chipangano," he says, shaking his head at me. "Don't move. I will deal with them."

There is angry shouting outside, and before the captain can

get to the door, it bursts open. Young men in green overalls carrying sticks and *shamboks* come shoving-pushing-shouting into the room. I have heard of the Youth Party, the Chipangano. Shadrack told me about them. He called them the Green Bombas. They wear green overalls and work for the president. Shadrack said that one day he would like to be one of them. If Shadrack was alive and could see them now, I think he would say it was a stupid idea.

The Green Bombas are all over the house. They must have followed us to Captain Washington's home.

7

THE GREEN BOMBAS

Who are you?"

"These are friends of mine...."

"Why are you not at the *pungwe*?"

"They are on their way...."

"Your dish is still on the wall!"

"I am taking it down...."

"Are you Chipangano? Where's your card?"

"No, I don't think..."

"Do you vote for the president?"

"The president is my president for life...."

"We are talking to these boys. Not you, Captain."

"These boys are not from Bikita."

"Who are they?"

"Friends of mine..."

"Are they MDC? Where are their Zed cards?"

"No! They are not MDC...."

"Where are their cards?"

Their words are like bullets. The room zings with their questions — they bounce off the walls, bounce off the ceiling. Innocent stands up and moves quickly behind me. I can feel him trembling. He hates questions he cannot answer. They confuse him. He ends up saying the wrong things. I say nothing to these boys. They are strong only because they are many. If I catch one of them alone, he will not have so many questions. Instead, he'll be worrying about how to stop his nose from bleeding and how to get my foot out of his ass.

I hold Innocent's hand tightly to show him that I am not afraid. Captain Washington is trying to answer them all at once, but they do not listen to him, they push at Innocent and me, wave their sticks in front of my face. Their eyes shine with anger. Their smiles are cruel. Grandpa Longdrop said you can always see a bully a mile away: he's the one who has a crowd around him and a smile on his face.

The house is too small for all of us. Some of them stand on the chairs; another has turned over the table. Two more Green Bombas have come through the kitchen door.

Captain Washington tries to block the leaders from getting to us. He pushes them back, shouts at them to leave us alone. They do not listen to him. None of these boys is older than Innocent, yet they do not listen to the best policeman in the district. What has happened to this place? Do the young people no longer respect their elders?

They poke Innocent with their sticks. He tries to swat their sticks away, but they laugh at him. Their laughter is hard, like plates breaking on a cement floor.

I can see what is happening. They want us to join them. We must become part of Chipangano. They want us to round up dissidents and take them to Commander Jesus. The commander wants more blood in his drums. He wants us to do his work for him, like the soldiers did in Gutu. They will take Innocent away with them and put him into green overalls. They'll turn him into a Green Bomba. They don't understand that he isn't like them. Without me, he will die.

Now I must think quickly. Captain Washington cannot help us now. He is no longer in control in his own house. I hate to do this to Innocent. He'll be angry with me afterward — very angry. But I have no choice. It is the only thing that will save us.

I put both my hands on my head and start chanting the old song that Grandpa Longdrop taught me, just as his grandmother taught him when he became a man. I feel Innocent freeze behind me. He did not understand the song nor its meaning, and when it was sung he lost himself. He was afraid then, to leave Amai, to leave his home, and the elders of the village decided that Innocent could remain uncut. Innocent never went into the bush to become a man.

"No, Deo!" he says, more frightened by what I am doing than of the Green Bombas. He knows what will happen to him.

The room falls silent. Everyone has heard the song and not heard the song. It is a song from long ago, from the old days. You think you know it, but you can't remember it until you hear it sung. The song is born in your bones — some can sing it, but few can understand it.

I am one who can sing it. I step forward. The Green Bombas stare at me, their sticks raised ready to strike. Amai used to sing all the time. Not this song, but others. I know each Green Bomba's *amai* did too. They know this song in their bones. I sing out loudly. Clap my hands together. Stamp my feet several times.

The song takes me over. My voice is no longer my own. It belongs to the song now. The Spirit song I sing will show them what Innocent really is.

I ignore the look on Captain Washington's face. I turn toward Innocent and sing to him. His eyes are wide as he watches me. He is still, staring at me, listening. He cannot ignore the song. His eyes start to roll in their sockets. He flicks his head back, and all that can be seen are the whites of his eyes. He lets out a growl. It is not a human sound. He moves forward, following the song. His head winds like a snake. He stands on his toes and lets his hands drop to his sides. He drops his jaw, and his mouth falls wide open. He growls again, shudders, and then groans.

Spit drips to the floor. His eyes roll in their sockets. He is lost to us now. The song has done its job.

It is always terrible to see Innocent when he has one of his fits. When he gets them it reminds me why I have to be with him, always. People are afraid of Innocent when he becomes like this. They think he is possessed. They think that the Spirits have taken over his body. They do not know what to do with the person that is not a person anymore. In my family we know how to deal with Innocent in these moments. They are only a part of who Innocent is.

The Green Bombas back away from Innocent. They are scared of him now. His face has changed. His lips twist and curl inside out. His eyebrows shoot up, then down again. He looks more animal than human.

I hate to do this to him. He will be exhausted for many days afterward. Grandpa Longdrop says that he lives four days in twenty minutes with all the muscles and energy he uses to keep himself from leaving us.

I stop singing.

My brother is lost to me now. I have pushed him into a place he hates to go more than anywhere else in the world. He no longer sees any of us in the room. Once I asked him what happens to him when he has a fit. Where does Innocent go? He said it was like seeing himself from a great height. That he looked down on his body and could do nothing about the terrible things it was doing. He said that sometimes he would like to just fly away, but he knew that if he left his body, it would die without him. He said he didn't want to be without a body. It was the only one he had. He said having a fit was like a bad dream that hurt him in his sleep. That is why Innocent always sleeps so well. He has no nightmares while he sleeps; he has them in the daytime for everyone to see.

Innocent drops to his knees. Soon he will collapse onto his side. I have only a few minutes before he is in danger of swallowing his tongue. This is when he needs me the most. I have to hold his head in my lap and stick my finger in his mouth to hold down his tongue.

"My brother is ill," I say into the faces of the Green Bombas. "He is crazy. A dog bit him." I lie, but I don't think Innocent will mind.

"Rabies!" cries one of the Green Bombas and steps back in fear.

I nod and look sad. "It's worse than rabies," I say. "He was born this way, but when the dog bit him it made him even crazier."

They have no reason not to believe me.

The Green Bombas are not smiling anymore. Nor are they angry anymore. They mumble, and some of them back away as if they are looking at a monster. They are nothing but stupid children afraid of a grown man who is having a fit on the kitchen floor. He can do them no harm, but still they are scared of him. The two Green Bombas who came in through the kitchen door have already run away. The others are backing out of the front door.

"Let's go. These boys are no use to us."

"We will be back to see you, Captain Washington."

"Make sure these two are gone when we come."

"Remember Operation Win or War."

The Green Bombas leave, and we are alone.

I have forgotten them already. I am with Innocent. I hold his head in my lap and force his tongue down. He tries to swallow, but my finger in his mouth stops him. I feel him go weaker. I stroke his head. The trembling slows. He sighs deeply, as if the nightmare is over. Slowly, Innocent returns from the land of his nightmare. He will be asleep soon. I rub his back in the way Amai used to do and feel his breathing becoming normal.

I don't know how long I've been sitting with Innocent, but when I look up I see Captain Washington at the table, drinking his booze and looking at me.

"You can do that to your brother?"

"I don't like to, but it was all I could think of."

He helps me carry Innocent to the couch. We cover him with a blanket. He is sleeping now as if someone had knocked him over the head.

"You can't stay here, Deo."

I've worked this out a long time ago. Of course we can't stay here. Other Green Bombas will come here and try to recruit Innocent. They will hurt him. I won't be able to play the same trick twice.

"I know."

"You must go to South Africa," he says. "It's the only safe place for Innocent. And for you too."

Go to South Africa. It is a thought bigger than what happened in Gutu, bigger than living in Bikita with Captain Washington, bigger than any thought I have ever had before.

"You can get a lift with one of the trucks. I know someone who can take you. He is leaving early tomorrow morning. The Green Bombas will come back," he says.

Captain Washington goes to the window and looks out on the street. Far away I can hear the sound of angry bees. I listen more carefully. It is not angry bees. It is chanting and the sound of drums beating somewhere in the night.

"That is the *pungwe*. I have to go. To not go is to suffer a beating. They have started, and they will go on through the night. You will be safe here. I will wake you and take you to the driver of the truck in the morning. You don't have any shoes?" he asks, looking at my bare feet.

I shake my head.

"I'll see what I can do. You can't go barefoot to South Africa."

Go to South Africa.

I nod at the captain. My tongue feels like a flat tire in my mouth.

Captain Washington drinks one more glassful of his booze and leaves. Innocent is snoring quietly on the couch. I listen to the chanting, the drums, the shouting. There is no sound like it — not angry bees, but angry people.

I gently lift Innocent's head and slip a cushion beneath it. I pull the curtains aside and look out onto the street. Empty. No one around. I feel I am the only person in Bikita. I go into Captain Washington's room and lie down on his bed. I look up at the ceiling. My mother used to come to this room and sit for hours and talk with the captain. I feel her spirit close to me now.

Go to South Africa, she says.

8

TRUCKING

I wake up with a headache. The truck cabin is hot and stuffy. Innocent's feet are up my nose, and they smell bad. I try to move them away, but there's no room in the sleeping cabin. Innocent grunts and shifts slightly. He is listening to his radio with a faraway look in his eyes. Around his neck is a pair of brand-new sneakers that Captain Washington gave us before we left. I quickly check that I still have my sneakers. I put them in one corner when we got into the truck at four o'clock this morning. They are where I left them — their new smell makes me smile. My soccer ball is in the other corner, still fat and round and stuffed full of money.

Captain Washington was almost crying when he hugged me good-bye early this morning, after helping me get Innocent up into the truck. I also wanted to cry.

"You'll be all right. South Africa is a better place than here," he said, handing me a new pair of white sneakers.

"When you get to Beitbridge, you must find Mai Maria. She will look after you. You'll be all right, you'll be all right."

I wished he would stop saying we'd be all right. He sounded like we wouldn't be. I remember Amai saying the same thing, and nothing was all right. The captain spoke very sternly to the driver about looking after us and making sure that we got safely to Beitbridge. The driver shrugged, nodded, threw down his cigarette, climbed up behind the steering wheel, drew the curtain of his cabin shut, and told us to go to sleep.

It didn't take long before we were driving out of Bikita, and then pretty soon we were fast asleep.

Now I pull open the curtain to the cabin behind the driver. The sun is bright. I check the clock on the dashboard — it is late morning. I must have slept for a long time. The truck driver is crouched over the steering wheel, staring at the road. Every now and then he blasts the horn at goats, children on the side of the road, or some slow car. He seems to be in a hurry to get to Beitbridge. He hands me a bottle of water.

"Stay behind the curtain," he grunts. "Military roadblock in ten minutes."

I drink from the bottle, hand it to Innocent. He turns off his radio and puts it away in his Bix-box. He drinks, hands back the bottle. I can see by the way he looks at me that he has something important to say.

"Are we going to see him?" he asks.

I don't know what he is talking about. Innocent takes out the photograph he showed me under the baobab tree. "Are we going to see him?" he asks again. "In Goodwood."

I look closely at the man hugging the boy Innocent. There is no chance that we can find him in South Africa. I wouldn't know where to begin to look for him.

"Yes," I say and hand him back the photograph. "We're going to see him in South Africa."

"See-aye-eight-three-two-seven-five-six-one-three," says Innocent.

"Huh?"

"The truck number," he says.

I ask him for the photograph again and look more closely at the picture. Amai, my father, and Innocent are standing in front of the truck. They are blocking the registration number.

"You remember the number of his truck?"

Innocent nods slowly.

Another thing about my brother: he eats numbers. Any number, anywhere, and in whatever order they come to him, he swallows them and never forgets them. He says numbers are his friends, and they run around in his brain like children. They make patterns in his head, and he likes to play with them. I don't know how he does it, but he can add and multiply faster than an electronic calculator. Grandpa Longdrop said that sometimes people like Innocent get extra gifts when they are born. With Innocent, it's numbers. Amai said it's what makes Innocent more special than anyone else.

"See-aye-eight-three-two-seven-five-six-one-three," he says again, pointing at the truck.

"Okay. Good. That will be easy then," I say, handing him back the photograph. That's the thing about Innocent, he's always got a surprise up his sleeve. Sometimes he can be a pain in the ass and a lot of hard work, but I'm very lucky to have him for a brother.

"And Grandpa Longdrop shouldn't complain to the president. I'm feeling a lot better now," he says.

"No, I'm sure he'll be very polite."

"The president is a very busy man. Lots of operations going on," he says, smiling.

The truck bumps as we go over another pothole. We bounce about on the bunk bed. Innocent hits his head. "Operation Fix the Road or Else," he says.

I shake my head at his joke and then laugh out loud. Innocent can do that to you, make you laugh until your sides hurt. He points at me, shaking his head. I have to wipe away the tears of laughter from my eyes.

The truck driver gears down. "Here's the roadblock," he says. "Stay hidden. Climb into the hole behind the bunk bed. Quickly!"

I pull the cushions to one side in the middle of the back section of the bunk. Behind the bunk bed is a small space. Innocent crawls through the back of the bunk first. I grab my soccer ball and the sneakers and follow him. The space smells of gas. There is barely room for one person. The driver shuts the panel. I hear him put back the cushions.

"Stay quiet!" he hisses. He sounds scared.

The engine of the truck is turned off.

On my side of the hiding place, there is a small hole that brings in a little light and air. My ears hum with the sudden silence after the noise of the engine. Innocent has both his fingers in his ears. His eyes are shut tight. He doesn't like the dark.

"Remember we don't want the soldiers to find us. They will take off your clothes again," I whisper to him. "We must keep very quiet."

I don't know if he hears me with his fingers in his ears, but at least he is still.

I peep through the hole. I can't see much — uniformed men, a small group of people with bags, parcels, and suitcases. I hear voices.

"Open up!"

The side of the truck is struck with something made of iron. Innocent jumps. I grip his arm to keep him quiet.

The driver is being questioned.

"Where are you going?"

"Beitbridge. Then Musina, then Polokwane."

"And inside?"

"Empty. I'm returning in two weeks with corn."

The doors of the back of the truck open. Somebody climbs in, thumps around, making a lot of noise in the empty truck. There are a few crashes as boxes are kicked around, over-turned. Each thump makes Innocent jump. He presses his fingers deeper into his ears.

"Shhh," I whisper very softly, stroking Innocent's arm. "It's going to be all right." I sound like Captain Washington.

The back door of the truck is slammed shut. I strain to hear what is being said, but the men have moved away.

I have to pee. I have to pee so badly. I cross my legs and squeeze. Peeing now would be very stupid. I imagine the sol-diers seeing my pee running from underneath the truck, mak-ing a little river at the soldiers' boots. I imagine them beating the driver, scrambling into the back of the cabin, and pulling us out of the hole. This thought makes me have to pee even more. I'm worried about Innocent. He won't last long in here.

Then I hear voices again, louder. Someone is groan-ing. Someone is pleading. The voices sound very frightened. Through the small hole I see a khaki uniform.

"What kind of shirt do you like to wear? Long sleeve or short sleeve?" This is one of the soldiers. He speaks loudly for all the people waiting around the truck to hear. It seems a funny question for a soldier to ask.

Nobody answers him.

"Answer!" he screams. "Long sleeve or short sleeve?"

I hear someone answer. It is a man's voice.

"Short sleeve," he says.

Why do they scream so? Why are the soldiers asking what type of shirts people want to wear? I look through the tiny hole.

Blood on the ground.

Commander Jesus must be collecting blood for his drums. They will find us. Take us to Commander Jesus. He will remember Innocent struck Commander Jesus's hand. We will die. I start to shiver. Innocent's eyes are wide with thousands of questions. I can no longer say it will be all right. It may not be.

The cabin door opens.

This is it.

Long sleeve or short sleeve? What will I answer?

I hear someone heave himself into the truck and sit down behind the wheel. The door slams shut. The engine roars into life.

We are moving slowly forward, moving through the roadblock. Then the driver shifts gears, and the truck picks up speed and rattles down the road. The driver must be in a hurry; we fly over potholes and get bumped around. The gas fumes fill up the space. Innocent starts coughing.

"It's done now, boys," says the driver.

I feel safe enough to push open the panel, and Innocent scrambles onto the bunk bed. I follow him and pull open the curtain.

"What happened? What happened back there?"

The driver looks gray. He shakes his head, slams his fist on the steering wheel. He does not answer me.

"I've got to pee," I shout over the noise.

"Pee in this," he says, handing me the water bottle. "I'm not stopping until we get to Beitbridge."

9

PATSON'S GAME

We arrive at Beitbridge late in the afternoon. I have never seen so many trucks in my life. They stand bumper to bumper, like a herd of great mechanical beasts waiting to cross the bridge. Their smaller cousins, cars and minibuses, are in a different line.

At the border town there are many strange sights: a small pickup truck has a load of furniture, bins, bicycles, and boxes covered by canvas — it looks like a giant snail. A man pushes a bicycle packed on both sides with boxes and suitcases that make it impossible for him to ride. Women push wheelbarrows piled with stuff. Rows of people sit in front of what they are trying to sell: herbs and roots, fruit, vegetables, medicines, postcards, batteries, plastic toys, CDs, suitcases. A man is cutting hair in one corner. A photographer takes photos against a grimy white board. And rows and rows of barbed-wire fences. And so many different people. People waiting; people leaving; people selling; people buying.

We climb out of the cabin, happy to stretch our legs. Innocent stands behind me. The noise and strangeness of the place make him uneasy.

"I need to eat and sleep now," says the driver. "The border is closed, and no one knows when it will open again. Maybe tonight, maybe tomorrow."

"What do we do?"

He shrugs. "Wait. See what happens when the border opens. Maybe you can come with me."

I don't believe him. He doesn't look at me. Instead he pulls some dollars from his pocket and hands them to me. "Get some food. Those women will help you." He points in the direction of the rows of women selling food. "Take your stuff. I want to sleep."

Maybe he doesn't want to be bothered with us anymore. I take the money, say thank you, and walk over to the sellers. Innocent follows me.

"You hungry?" I ask.

He nods. He holds his Bix-box under his right arm. His white sneakers dangle around his neck. I glance back at the truck. The driver watches us. He lifts his hand. I think he might be saying good-bye, but I can't be sure. He climbs back into the truck, slams the door.

We buy some chicken and pap and warm Fanta. I have to use a little of the money from the soccer ball but not much. We sit to one side and eat our feast. Innocent hums while he eats. It's a sign that he is happy. Afterward, I look more closely at the people. Many of them have children with them, girls and boys my age.

Innocent picks up the soccer ball and tosses it to me. He knows what I am thinking.

"Play, Deo. I'll watch you. Don't worry."

I take off my sneakers and leave them with him. The soccer ball feels good on my bare feet. I kick the ball into the clearing, toss it up onto my knee, and bounce it a few times, before letting it land on my foot. I balance it there for a moment and then flick it up into the air onto my forehead. With two headers, I let the ball back to the ground and place my foot over it and look up.

Out of the hordes of people going about their business, a few watch me. The watchers stand out from the adults who are always talking, moving about, not aware of their children. The boys watch me, their eyes on my ball. They are like me. One of them steps forward. He stops a few paces away and waits.

I kick the ball to him.

He stops it with his foot and kicks it back right away. Another boy steps forward and calls out something I do not understand. His skin is like shiny coal. I kick the ball to him. He laughs as the ball sails toward him. He sticks out his chest and bumps the ball back to the ground and without looking up kicks it straight back to me.

More boys leave their families. Soon there are ten, eleven, no, twelve of them standing awkwardly around. Waiting.

The boy with the skin of coal says, "Aziz Mohammed. We play?"

I turn to the other boys and point to one of them. He is tall, looks strong. He will make a good defender. He runs over.

"Mujuru," he says. I guess it's his name.

I turn to Aziz. "My name's Deo."

He grins at me and looks carefully at the boys standing around. He points at a lean, wiry boy. "You. Sinbaba." The boy called Sinbaba trots over and stands next to Aziz.

I choose. He chooses. And so it goes on until everyone who has shown interest is part of the game. Then, standing to one side, I see the boy with the crutches and the one leg. I remember him from the baobab tree. His people must also have been heading for the border. He steps forward as if he has made up his mind. Thirteen pairs of eyes turn toward him. Surely he can't expect to play with us? He digs his crutches into the dirt and comes closer. There is a fire in his eyes. His mouth is a hard, determined line in a face of stone.

Nobody moves.

He digs his crutches into the dirt again and takes another step forward. He is staring at me, daring me. How does this boy think he can play with only one leg? I feel sorry for him, but he can't play with us.

He stares at me as if he can read my thoughts. Then he jerks his head backward, lifting one of his crutches in the air as if he is calling for something. I don't know what makes me do it, but I throw the ball toward him. He lurches forward, plants both his crutches, swings forward with his good leg, and kicks the ball so hard that it sails over our heads. Sinbaba jumps and catches it.

"I'll take you," I say. He doesn't smile or thank me but moves to my side as if this is what he expected.

Some of the boys are from Zimbabwe, and their names are familiar, but others are from Senegal, Democratic Republic of Congo, and Angola.

Before we begin, I bring my team together.

"Mujuru, you play central defender." He nods, and I turn to the two younger boys from Angola. They look fast. "You two play on left and right wing, you two at midfield, and the two of us"—I point at a boy who is my height and looks equally strong—"are the strikers."

"Fantan," the boy says. "My name's Fantan."

"Okay, and you?" I turn to the boy with the crutches.

"Patson," he says. "I play goalie."

"Where you from, Patson?" I ask, recognizing his accent.

"Masvingo Province" is all he says, swinging away swiftly to our goal.

"Let's play!" calls Aziz.

The game is on.

At first the play is scrappy. Everyone is hungry to feel leather against skin. They all run after the ball like bees after the queen bee. We pack around the ball and kick at dust. It doesn't make sense. There is no discipline. It's typical of a game with newcomers—everyone wants to show what he can do.

Aziz is easily the best player on his side. He quickly dribbles through the crowd, pushing for the ball, and before anyone on my team knows it, he has passed to Sinbaba, who taps it back to him, and Aziz easily shoots past Patson. Nobody could have saved that shot. These two have obviously played together. They jog back to their half, talking in their own language.

I call my guys together. "Stay in your position. Mark one of their team. Don't run after the ball. Wait for it to come to you."

We start again. It's only a little better. There are one or two good passes, but Aziz and Sinbaba are lethal. They swoop down like falcons when the ball goes loose, and before Mujuru can do anything to block them, they glide past him and another perfect shot at goal is soaring past Patson.

At the second goal, I notice that some of the adults are watching us now. Some of the older men have gathered on the side, cheering on the boys they know and shouting instructions. I glance over at Innocent. He sees me and raises his hand. His radio is pressed to his ear, and he's grinning.

I focus on Aziz. There is some trick that he does with the ball that I haven't worked out yet. As he comes toward you he sort of jumps over the ball and then twists it around his ankle, and before you know it, he's past you and the ball is at his feet. I run toward him, keeping my eye on the ball. He sees me approach, keeps his head down, and dances around me as easy as spinning a coin. I'm left eating his dirt as he runs past. I charge him from behind and deliberately kick his ankles. He falls, and the players on his team shout at me. Sinbaba walks up.

"That's a foul."

I glare at him. He knows he's right.

Aziz gets up, inspects his knee. It's bloody.

"That's a penalty, Deo," he says, rubbing his knees. He is angry but in control.

Fantan runs over. "Who cares? Let's play on."

"No!" says Aziz. "That's a penalty and he knows it."

I stare him down. It's no use. I know I am wrong.

"Penalty," I agree and walk toward Patson. The fire is still burning in his eyes. I want to say to him that since I made the mistake, I should try to save the goal, but I can see he will not allow it.

The boys stand around while Patson makes himself ready for the penalty. Aziz marks out the distance and places the ball on the ground. There is some argument about where the penalty should be taken from, but at last we all agree on where the spot should be. I quickly check the twine that is holding the ball together. My homemade soccer ball is doing pretty well.

I toss the ball to Aziz, who places the ball on the spot. He takes a few steps back and eyes Patson. I know what he is thinking: This will be easy. Patson stretches out his arms, balancing on one leg. His outstretched crutches almost cover the entire goal. I notice all around the pitch, people have paused in their business to see the outcome of the kick.

Aziz runs up to make the kick. He feints left, but Patson does not move. The ball flies quickly to his right, heading for the top corner. Patson times it sweetly. He dives to the right and pokes at the ball with the end of his crutch. It lands at his feet, and with one quick hop, he places his crutches on the ground and gives the ball an almighty kick. Fantan collects the ball and passes it swiftly to my right foot. I transfer it to my left and slip past Sinbaba before sending it straight through the empty goal.

My team goes crazy. Innocent runs up and down. "*Goooaaal*," he shouts.

I run back to Patson. "Good save!" I say.

He grins for the first time, and the game is back on.

There are more people around the pitch now, and I hear a bit of applause and a few shouts of encouragement. Patson's save has motivated our team. They attack the goal, and before Aziz and Sinbaba know what has happened, Fantan has slipped past the defense and has scored a goal from a long pass from center field.

We play until the insects are buzzing around the tall, tall lights of the border post and the night has crept up on Beitbridge. All is forgotten as the ball moves from player to player, foot to head, head to goal.

In this moment I am all I ever want to be. I am free of worry, released from fear, unable to think of anything but this moment. I fly from one side of the pitch to the next, I weigh up my opponents, test their weaknesses, wait for an opening, calculate the flight of the ball, guess what my team-mates will do next. There is no yesterday or the night before; there is no tomorrow or the day after that. There is only now: a soccer ball, players running from side to side, and the goal at the end of the pitch.

It is so good to be running, to call on my speed when I need it to outrun plodding Sinbaba or to pass lightning-fast Aziz. On the side, Innocent is walking up and down as he always does when I play. Every time I get the ball and slip past a player I can hear him.

"Goooooo Deo!" he shouts.

The score has become unimportant. It could be 7-6 or maybe 9-8. None of us is interested in winning, just playing. After about an hour we take a break and drink from the tap behind the office buildings. I splash the water over my face and drink thirstily.

"Aziz, you have to show me that move of yours," I say, tossing him the ball as we walk back to the pitch. He demonstrates it in slow motion. I try it out. It will take a lot of practice to get it right.

We play for another hour, but the game is different now. One or two of the boys are called back by their mothers, and I can see that the others are tired. I look up to see what Innocent is doing. He sits on the ground, legs crossed in front of him, listening to his radio. I must remember to get some batteries before we cross into South Africa.

Which makes me think about our truck and driver.

The line of trucks is moving. The mechanical beasts are on the move. While we were playing, they must have opened the border and allowed the trucks to go through.

I grab my ball. "I've got to go."

I run over to Innocent, haul him up from the ground, and run to where our truck was parked.

It's gone.

I run down the line of trucks, trying to find him. There is no sign of our truck. The driver has left us behind.

"Look at the lights, Deo. They're so big. So bright. It's like daytime."

Innocent is staring up at the lights towering over the border post. He turns slowly, hypnotized by their brightness. I look around the border post. People are still waiting, still sitting around in groups. I spot a place under a tree a little distance from the building. It's as good a place as anywhere.

"Come on," I say, "let's go and sleep. Tomorrow we have to look for Mai Maria."

We walk over to the tree, but on the way Aziz and Sinbaba run up. "You come with us. You can't sleep there," Aziz says.

"There are many robbers here," Sinbaba says, jerking his head at a group of men moving slowly through the crowd. "It's not good to sleep by yourself, especially when you have so much money."

Sinbaba points to the soccer ball. So he noticed what it was stuffed with. I hold it close to me.

"Robbers?" says Innocent, looking frightened.

"My brother doesn't like robbers."

"Don't worry. Come," says Aziz.

We walk back to where Aziz and his family have been camping before trying to cross into South Africa. They have been waiting for two days. There is something wrong with their papers. Aziz tries to explain, but I catch only every second or third word. He speaks strangely. They are Muslim. His father wears a hat, and his mother has a scarf around her head. The father laughs when I show him my ball.

"Aziz says he wants one just like it," he says, handing it back to me. "You are welcome, Deo. You can sleep there. Mama, give the boys a *dhoti* to sleep on and some sweet chai before they sleep."

Aziz's mother hands out thin sheets, and we are each given mats to sleep on. It's better than lying on the ground.

10

FINDING MAI MARIA

When I wake up in the morning there are twice as many people at Beitbridge as the night before. It is as if the whole of Zimbabwe has arrived for the opening of the border. The air crackles with energy; people are moving about; the mamas are laying out their goods; people are jostling in the queue, getting ready for another day of waiting. Aziz and his family pack up their belongings and hurry to join the long line of people in front of the office. The place where we played soccer last night has become a noisy taxi stand. Minibuses park side by side, and their drivers and number twos are busy loading and unloading passengers, fixing tires, cleaning their windshields, and trying to out-shout one another to get fares.

"Pay forward!" they shout. "Pay forward!"

"Musina. Polokwane. Pay forward!"

"Air-conditioning! Fast like lightning!"

"Pay forward! Pay forward!"

I ask Aziz what this means.

"You get a lift with them once you have your papers, and then you pay on the other side," he answers.

"Many people don't have the money on this side," explains his father, "so the taxi drivers allow you to pay once you get to your people."

"And how much is it to take one of those taxis to South Africa?"

"Two thousand rands," he answers.

I don't know what that means in Zim dollars.

"Two hundred billion Zim dollars," he says.

But who can afford that! I don't have two hundred billion dollars, and there is no one on the other side who will give me rands. Pay forward is not for us.

I have to find Mai Maria. As Aziz and his family move away, I ask them if they have heard of Mai Maria. Aziz's father shakes his head and points to some of the women selling food.

"Ask them. They know everything that happens here," he says, hurrying his family away. Aziz looks back at me, waving good-bye.

"Thanks for the move, Aziz," I shout after him, but he is swept away by the crush of people heading for the immigration office.

Finding Mai Maria is not as difficult as I thought it would be. Everyone at the border town of Beitbridge knows her. The women point me to a well-worn path that leads away from the border into the bush beyond a barbed-wire fence.

"Careful she doesn't eat you up," one of the women warns, and the others cackle with laughter at the look on Innocent's face. "She's a witch, that one. Be careful, *wena*!"

I follow the path, and Innocent stumbles after me.

"What did they say, Deo? Who's a witch?" Innocent hates stories about witches and cannibals. "Where are we going, Deo? I don't want to see the witch, Deo."

"They were just making a joke — trying to be clever. Don't listen to them."

"Mai Maria is a bad woman. They said so. I do not want to see her. Innocent stays here."

He stops walking.

"Listen, Innocent, we do not have the money to take a taxi, and our truck driver has left without us. Remember what Captain Washington said? We have to find Mai Maria."

"But she's a witch! I don't want to find her," he says angrily.

"You want to get to South Africa, right?" I shout at him. "You want to find your dad, right? Well, you're not going to find him on this side of the border. We have to get across to the other side, and Mai Maria is going to help us. So do what you want to do!" I know I am being tough on him, but sometimes it's the only way.

"Yes," he says. "That's true, but if she's a witch…"

I tune him out as I follow the path, which leads us down to the banks of the Limpopo River. The river is a slow-moving silver ribbon. I don't see another bridge this way. Perhaps Mai Maria has a boat that takes people across the river? We walk on for another hour. Innocent is trailing, mumbling, but I pay him no attention. We follow the path, and Innocent points out several crocodiles lying in the sun on the mud bank of the river. Even from here I can see that they are huge. Of course the Limpopo River has crocodiles, I remind myself, but how did they get to be so fat?

Crocodiles or witches? I know which one I would choose.

"No soccer today, Deo?" Innocent has caught up and is walking close behind me.

"Today we go to South Africa," I answer. He is trying to make up for being so pig-headed earlier, and there's no point in staying angry with him. He forgets arguments as soon as we've had them. "Look across the Limpopo River, Innocent. That's South Africa."

"There we will find my dad," he says.

"Sure we will," I say, even though I don't know where we will go when we get to the other side. Or what we'll do. After hearing how much the taxis cost, I don't want to spend any more of our money. I have a hollow feeling in my stomach; I don't think we have nearly enough money.

After an hour of walking we come to a clearing with several small huts, a little way from the Limpopo River. We stop and look around. There is no one about. The huts are empty and swept clean, but in the middle of the clearing there is a smoldering fire. Next to it is a large black pot, which has been turned over. My stomach grumbles. We've had nothing to eat this morning. I check inside the pot—burned pap at the bottom. I scrape off as much as I can, and Innocent and I sit down to a breakfast of cold, blackened pap.

"AND WHAT DO YOU THINK YOU'RE DOING?"

A voice booms in the clearing, and I jump up. Storming toward me is the ugliest, fattest, angriest woman I have ever seen. I swallow as fast as I can, drop the crust back into the pot, and stare at this enormous woman shaking her fist at me. The fat in her upper arm is going into a speed wobble. She has a head of dreadlocks like thick black mamba snakes. A scar runs from her forehead over her nose to the corner of her mouth. I see flashes of gold in her mouth.

"BY JAH! YOU HAVE SOME NERVE SITTING AT MY FIRE, EATING MY FOOD, AND SNOOPING AROUND. I'LL FEED YOU TO THE VULTURES!"

I want to stick my fingers into my ears to block the force of her words, but I doubt that that will stop this woman. She looks exactly like a witch. Her bare feet are like blocks of cement, and she wears bright red shorts that barely cover her fat thighs. Her breasts hang dangerously loose behind her T-shirt, moving about like a pair of snuffling anteaters.

"YOU ROBBERS! YOU DOGS! YOU LIONS OF ZIMBO! WHAT DO YOU THINK YOU'RE DOING HERE?" One loose eye moves around in its socket with a life of its own. The other is staring at me as steady as a hawk's eye. All I want to do is turn around and run for my life.

But then Innocent does a funny thing. He grabs my wrist

and pulls me behind him. He is trembling with the effort of facing this woman.

"Stand where you are, witch!" he says loudly. "You will not eat us. We have not come here to be eaten."

Her single hawk eye focuses on Innocent. "WHAT ARE YOU SAYING?" she booms.

"You will not eat Deo. He is my little brother. If you want to eat someone, it will have to be me." Innocent's voice trembles, but he does not back down in the face of this horrible woman.

The woman lets out a roar. She slaps her man-sized hands together, throws her head back, and stamps her foot. Her black mambas swirl around her shoulders as if they've seen a mongoose. I'm not sure whether she's angry, laughing, or choking to death.

"Who would want to eat you?" she asks, spluttering and wheezing, pointing at Innocent and then slapping her hands together.

"The witch called Mai Maria eats people," says Innocent boldly.

"I am Mai Maria, boy! But I don't eat people."

"If you are Mai Maria, you will take us across the river," he says. "I need to find my father. He is over there."

"Aha! You want to make a crossing." She wipes tears from her eyes. "Who told you about Mai Maria?"

"Captain Washington," I say, stepping from behind my brother.

Mai Maria's single steady eye focuses on me.

"My friend, Captain Washington? You boys have come from Masvingo Province? From Bikita?"

"Yes. From Gutu," I say.

"I've heard what happened in Gutu. Terrible, too terrible. And now you want to go over to the other side. Do you know how much I charge to take people to South Africa?"

I shake my head.

"Two hundred rands—today that is twenty billion Zim dollars. Tomorrow it might be thirty billion. You'd better go today."

My heart sinks. We haven't enough money, but I pick up my soccer ball and untie the twine. Mai Maria watches with interest as I pile all our money on the ground in front of her and start counting. It's not even close to ten billion, and I know Mai Maria knows it too.

"So, you are the boy with the soccer ball? I heard about the game last night. You chose the boy with one leg to be on your team?"

I nod at her and stand up.

"You will see that boy later on today. He comes here with his father. They will make the crossing tomorrow."

I nod again, not knowing what to say. It seems Captain Washington was right. Mai Maria knows everything about getting people across the border.

"Okay. I tell you what we do. You two are special. The boy with a billion-dollar soccer ball and the crazy brother who thinks Mai Maria eats children. I like you two. We make a deal. You give me your money and those sneakers, and I'll take you over to South Africa. This must be our secret. You tell no one how cheap it is to cross, okay? Otherwise they will all think Mai Maria has gone soft."

Innocent clutches the sneakers around his neck. He hasn't worn them even once since Captain Washington gave them to him. I can see this will be trouble.

"Let me talk to him." I pull Innocent a few steps away from the fire.

"The witch can't have my sneakers, Deo."

"You want to get across, right? You want to see Dad? This is the only way," I whisper urgently.

"Why isn't our money enough? We're giving all of it to her. That should be enough."

"It's not enough, Innocent. That's just the way it is. And it will be no use to us over there, anyway. They have different money across the river."

"But the captain gave those sneakers to me...."

"I'll get you another pair on the other side, exactly the same. I promise."

"Promise?"

"Promise."

"Okay, you've got a deal," I say, walking back to Mai Maria, giving her our sneakers.

She snorts again, inspecting the shoes, sniffing the inner soles. She gathers up the money, and it disappears somewhere under her clothes. I fold up my soccer-ball-no-more and place it under my shirt.

"Now you are the guests of Mai Maria for a day and half a night. More people will come, and by tonight there will be many here. They will sit around the fire and sing songs and say good-bye to their land. You will see," she says, snorting and shaking with laughter again. "As you are my first customers, you can have the pick of the huts. That is where you will sleep tonight, and tomorrow morning, when it is dark and the crocodiles are sleeping, we will cross the river."

11

CROCODILES IN THE LIMPOPO

I am dreaming of Amai. She touches my cheek and smiles at me. Amai's face hovers over me, close, the tiny wrinkles around her eyes reminding me of her laughter. I reach out to hug her, but she is shaking me, shaking me awake.

And then I open my eyes, awake now, with only the pain of missing her.

It is still dark.

In the hut there are the sounds and smells of people sleeping close to one another. A bird sings its early morning call. The murmur of people talking outside drifts into the hut. I reach out for Innocent.

He is no longer sleeping beside me. I sit up, instantly awake. I must find Innocent. What if he went wandering during the night? Sometimes Innocent goes on a walkabout and then cannot find his way back home. In this strange place, it would be easy for him to walk back to Beitbridge and then be unable to find his way back to Mai Maria's place.

I step over the bodies of sleeping people to get to the entrance.

A man swears at me. I've bumped his head. I don't care. I must get out of the hut and find Innocent. Today's the day we cross into South Africa. We have only one chance. If he has disappeared, I will have to stay behind to find him, and we will lose what we paid to Mai Maria.

Outside the hut, a fire is burning at the center of the clearing, and steam rises from a big black pot. Innocent is in deep conversation with Patson. Last night these two became good friends, when Innocent asked Patson about his leg, not pretending he was like everyone else. He even allowed Patson to listen to music on his radio, and that is something I've never been allowed to do.

At the thought of last night, I quickly glance around at the other two huts. The men from Harare are not around. The clearing is quiet. A few people come out of the hut, stretch, wash their faces from a tap behind Mai Maria's hut, and gather their belongings, ready for the crossing. Last night I heard many stories of the dangers ahead of us today. People spoke about the Ghuma-ghuma, but I didn't understand what it was. I heard something about crossing a park and how people had died trying. I don't want to believe them, but the adults spoke in such serious tones it's hard not to worry.

And then a fight broke out around the campfire. Three men and two women from Harare started shouting for beer and then complained to Mai Maria about how expensive it was. There was an ugly moment when one of the men swore into her face. He called her a filthy Rasta woman. Mai Maria said nothing. She stood with her hands on her hips and looked at him in a way that would keep me awake for weeks. When everyone started shouting and swearing, I pulled Innocent away and went to the sleeping hut. I was tired of trouble.

I walk over to where Innocent and Patson are sitting. A man makes tea and hands out slices of buttered bread. Above the huts the faintest light of the day rises, but it is still dark in the clearing.

"There will be no crocodiles where we cross," says Innocent to me, moving up on the log to make room for me. "Patson says so."

I sip at my tea and catch Patson's eye. He knows what I am thinking. There will be thirty-two people making the crossing today. How many will make it?

"My father will have to carry me some of the way," he says bitterly. "He promised Mai Maria that I would not hold up everyone. I won't."

It's hard not to stare at where his leg should be, so I look up instead. There are more and more people coming out of the huts. The men from Harare and the two women are the last to come out. They grumble when they get cold tea and have to share the last of the bread. Mai Maria is nowhere to be seen.

"We leave in ten minutes," one of Mai Maria's helpers calls to everyone standing around the fire. We finish our tea and collect our belongings.

Patson's father comes over to us. He is a tall man but doesn't look like he is strong enough to carry Patson across the river. He has a large backpack on his back, and he puts out his hand to Patson, who grabs it and lifts himself up onto his crutches.

"You're ready?" he asks.

"Ready," says Patson, throwing the last of his tea into the fire. The water sizzles instantly. It's as if he is throwing away all the memories of this place. "And you two?"

"We are crossing today. We're coming with you."

"And once you're on the other side, what will you do then?" Patson asks.

I shrug. It's a question I have been trying not to think about. "Something will come up," I say.

We move out of the clearing and follow a steep path to the Limpopo River. At first the sound of the river is a long way off, but as we get closer, the water sounds louder and louder.

"Will we see the witch again?" asks Innocent.

"I don't know. Keep walking and watch your step."

Innocent doesn't have great balance, and getting him down the steep trail is not easy. If he trips, he will grab at anyone to keep upright. He could bring the whole line of people tumbling down the path. Ahead of us, people walk single file down the trail, slowly making their way to the cold, gray river below.

I shiver at the sight of the fast-moving water. When I asked last night how we would cross the river, one man said, "Why, we're going to walk across," and the others laughed at his joke, which I didn't catch. Now, I look at the other side—surely this isn't the place that we cross. It will be too far!

Mai Maria's helpers jump from rock to rock and move steadily along the bank of the river. They look like they know where they are going, and we follow them as closely as we can. Patson and his father struggle behind us. Every time we cross over rocks, Patson's father has to swing his backpack in front of him and half drag, half carry Patson over the rocks. I offer to take the backpack, but he refuses.

We scramble over some rocks and turn a corner, and there, sitting on a rock overlooking the river, is Mai Maria. She has obviously been waiting for us.

"Across the river is South Africa," she begins. "On the other side there will be others who will lead you through the park. Listen to them carefully. Your life may depend on it. They have done this many times. You will need to do it only once." Her voice is as loud as always and easily carries over the noise of the river.

I look across to South Africa. It looks the same as Zimbabwe—same bushes, same trees, same sky. Everyone talks about the opportunities of good work with good pay. A better life there, they say, than in Zimbabwe. It's hard to imagine anything better than my life in Gutu before the soldiers came, but I have lived for only fourteen years.

"It looks deep," says Innocent. "Where's the bridge that bites, Deo?"

He is nervous because he can't swim. "We left Beitbridge behind, Innocent. You'll be okay."

"Each of you will hold on to the stick with your right hand," says Mai Maria, as her helpers pull long bamboo poles from behind the rocks. Rope knots have been tied at regular intervals on the poles. We are divided up into groups of six or seven people per pole. Innocent becomes even more frightened as he watches what is happening. He starts shaking his head from side to side.

I don't know how I am going to get Innocent across the Limpopo River. The banks on the other side seem impossibly far away.

"Do not let go of the pole! If you do, you will be swept away by the river toward the crocodiles you saw on your way here. Keep your feet on the riverbed and drag yourself through the water. If you lift your feet too high, the water will take you," says Mai Maria, as the three men from Harare and their two women push their way to the front of the group to take the first pole.

They swear at Mai Maria and tell her helper that it's time to go. Mai Maria simply looks at them. I see her exchange a glance with the lead helper as one by one the three men follow him into the water, while the two women moan to each other about how cold the water is.

Above us, a golden light grows in the east, and the tops of the trees gather color with the first thin rays of sunlight. Down by the river, the light is still gray and it is not yet fully morning.

I watch the first group carefully.

The helper walks steadily through the water, dragging his feet and holding on to the front of the pole. The water curls up around his lower legs. The women shriek as the water rises up around their legs. The current is strong, but the river is not deep. Then one of the women slips, her head disappearing under the water.

"DON'T LET GO!" bellows Mai Maria.

The man behind grabs her and she comes out of the water, spluttering and coughing. She starts walking again, and they continue on into the middle of the river. The second group heads into the shallow water.

Innocent is shivering in terror behind me. "No, Deo, Innocent doesn't want to do this. Let's go home. This is no good. No good at all," he says, pulling my arm.

I understand what Innocent is feeling, and I feel it too. Perhaps this is a big mistake. What if he slips and the river sweeps him toward the waiting crocodiles? How will I live with myself if Innocent drowns?

What if *I'm* swept away by the river? Who will look after Innocent if I drown?

The helpers are preparing for the third group to cross. Mai Maria is shouting instructions. We could slip away; nobody will notice if we are not here. We could run back up the slope and go back to the border. There has to be another way of crossing into South Africa.

"Innocent, will you help me?" This is Patson. He stands in

front of us and holds out his crutches to Innocent. "My father has to carry me on his back. It is the only way. I cannot get across without your help." Patson stares at me, as if he knows what is going through my mind. "Deo, don't leave now. You can make it. I know you can."

What does he know about me, and what I can or cannot do? How did he know what I was thinking?

"You can make it," he says again. "Look."

The first group is almost at the mud bank on the other side. Although they still have a way to go, they've made it through the deeper part of the river.

Innocent grabs Patson's crutches and stumbles forward. Helping Patson is all that matters to him now.

"Come down here, Lennox!" Mai Maria blasts from her rock. "I want you to look after these three boys. No trouble for them, hey?" she says, pointing her finger at a tall man who waits for us. "The Ghuma-ghuma can take the first lot, but these three — you look after them."

Lennox nods at her. I want to ask about the Ghuma-ghuma, but something tells me that now is not the time. Lennox takes the crutches from Innocent and lashes them to the bamboo pole. Patson's father holds on to the first knot and lifts his son onto his back, holding his butt with his left hand. Patson wraps his leg around his father's waist and clings to his neck. Patson's father has the backpack strapped to his chest. He doesn't look very comfortable.

Innocent grabs hold of the pole with his right hand. I take

his Bix-box and stuff it into a plastic bag I found. Behind me, two more men take their place at the remaining knots on our pole. At the end is another one of Mai Maria's helpers. We start moving toward the water. There is no turning back now.

"HEY, SOCCER BOY, WHEN YOU GET INTO THE PARK, DON'T STOP RUNNING. YOU HEAR ME? NOT FOR ANYTHING!" I hear Mai Maria yell, but I'm not sure what she means.

I have to get Innocent across the Limpopo River. The water is cold. The current tugs at my ankles. Innocent whimpers in fear in front of me.

"Drag your feet, Innocent, don't lift them out of the water," I say.

"Nobody must let go!" shouts Lennox from the front. "The water may pull you, but you must not let go of the pole."

We wade into the river, deeper into the mud. I stub my toe on a rock. The water covers my knees. I wrap my right arm around the pole and cling to the rope knot.

"Hold tight, Innocent. Hold tight!" I shout.

"I'm holding, I'm holding," cries Innocent.

The water claws at my thighs. It wants to pull me down-river to where the crocodiles wait. I lift the plastic bag above my head, trying to keep my balance. We are not yet in the middle, and the water is already lapping at my stomach. If it gets any deeper, I won't be able to hold on.

Then Innocent slips. The water sweeps him off his feet but he holds on to the pole with both hands.

"Don't let go!" shouts Lennox.

"Let him go! He will take us all down!" bellows the man behind me.

"No! Innocent, you must hold on!"

We stop moving. I cannot help Innocent without letting go of the pole and dropping the damn Bix-box. Lennox has now turned completely around and is trying to move past Patson's father to help Innocent. I hear the splashing of somebody coming through the water. The last man at the back of the pole has rushed forward.

"Grab him!" he shouts.

Patson slides off his father's back and tries to help Innocent.

"No, Patson!" shouts his father, but it is too late. Patson is in the water, struggling to get Innocent back onto his feet.

Innocent disappears under the water.

He thrashes about, trying desperately to get a grip. His face breaks the surface of the water. A wave covers him again. He's spluttering and coughing. "Deo, help me! Help me!"

I try to lift him up, but he is too heavy for me. I'm losing my grip on the pole. From behind, Mai Maria's helper wraps one arm around Innocent's chest and somehow pulls him out of the water. Innocent's hands are locked on to the pole, making it difficult for the man to get him upright.

"Let go with your left hand!" I shout at him. "Stand up, Innocent. Stand up!"

He tries to stand up. "Deo, I'm slipping. I'm slipping," he

screams in terror. But the man jerks him roughly into an upright position.

"Move!" the man shouts at Lennox.

Lennox turns around and starts moving toward the faraway riverbank. Patson's father is struggling to hold on to Patson, who is holding on to Innocent, who is holding on to the man.

"Patson, let him go! I've got him now," shouts the man. "Hold on to the pole."

Every now and then Patson kicks with his leg and then sinks back into the water. His father has lifted the pole above the water and is dragging and lifting at the same time. Innocent is still whimpering but is able to drag himself through the water now that the man is holding him up.

My legs ache. Cramps stab my thighs. I don't know how much longer I can hold on to the pole. The other side still seems so far away.

"We're almost there, Innocent. Keep going. Take one step at a time. Almost there," I say to encourage both of us.

And then suddenly, the river lets us go into shallow waters, the water lapping gently at our ankles. We scramble up the bank of the river and collapse on the ground. We've made it across the Limpopo River and into South Africa.

"Hurry! No rest now," shouts Lennox. "The Ghuma-ghuma will come. The danger is not over."

If he has done this so many times, why does he sound so afraid?

12

GHUMA-GHUMA

Lennox runs up the riverbank and sprints toward the nearest bushes. I don't know what is going on. We are here in South Africa now — what is there to be afraid of? Patson's father struggles to his feet and frantically tries to untie Patson's crutches from the bamboo pole. The water has made the knots tight, and he can't get the crutches free.

"Wait!" he shouts after Lennox. "My son needs them."

The two men who crossed the river with us run after Lennox. Neither will help Patson.

"In my Bix-box," says Innocent. "In my Bix-box."

I give him his tin box. Innocent takes out a pocketknife and hands it to Patson's father. The string binding the crutches is quickly cut, and Patson slips the crutches under his arms and negotiates his way over the rocks.

I look up and down the riverbank. The groups that crossed ahead of us have disappeared into the bush. The men and women from Harare, however, rest on the rocks of the riverbank. One of the women is complaining loudly and wringing out water from her skirt. The men smoke cigarettes, enjoying the morning sun. There are no signs of Mai Maria's men who took them across the river.

Then, without warning, from out of the bush, a group of men appears above the rocks. One of them carries a rifle in his hands as if it is nothing, as if its power is asleep. The men who walk with him all carry heavy sticks and machetes. The group smoking and laughing on the rocks beside the river has not yet noticed these men.

"Ghuma-ghuma," whispers Mai Maria's helper. "Hurry! They must not find us here. Big trouble. Come!"

Patson hobbles after his father, his crutches slipping in the river mud. As Innocent scrambles up the bank, I watch the Ghuma-ghuma moving over the rocks toward the group from Harare.

"What do they want?"

"Everything you have," comes the answer.

The Ghuma-ghuma fall upon the group from Harare. Machetes and sticks are raised in the air; the men try to run away. The women cry out for mercy. They are trapped between the river and the Ghuma-ghuma. They have been led right into the hands of robbers.

Innocent stops and turns around. He wants to see the reason for all the noise. I push him up the riverbank. "Go! Run, Innocent. Run!"

We dive into the bushes. Rough hands pull me down. It is Lennox.

"Lie still! Not a word. Keep quiet or they will find us," he hisses, pushing Patson's father farther back into the bushes. "You." Lennox points at Innocent. "Shut up or I will cut off your balls."

I pull Innocent down. And not a moment too soon.

Ghuma-ghuma rush up to where we stood a moment ago. Two of them carry the bags of the men from Harare. Now I understand what the adults were whispering about last night. These men are waiting for people who have crossed the Limpopo. The Ghuma-ghuma wait to beat and rob them. It's so easy.

Lennox is breathing softly beside me. He is watching closely, holding a big knife in his hand. I hold tightly on to Innocent's arm. He knows of the danger. He has his fingers in his ears and has closed his eyes.

The Ghuma-ghuma look up and down the path. The man with the rifle kneels and checks our footprints in the sand. He looks up and stares in our direction.

I hold my breath. Lennox is rock-still.

But then one of the men notices another group crossing farther up the river. He shouts to the man with the rifle, and the Ghuma-ghuma run down toward the river to attack their next victims. The man with the rifle follows.

"Now!" whispers Lennox. "Let's go."

We slip out of the bushes and start running.

Patson jumps onto his father's back. Innocent follows Lennox and I run behind him. The two men follow me. We can hardly keep up with Lennox. I feel a pain in my side — the running-too-fast-too-long pain. After a while Lennox slows down. In front of us is a huge barbed-wire fence.

"This is the first park. There is great danger beyond this fence. We must run now for two hours."

"A game reserve," says Patson's father. "It's a place with wild animals?"

"Or you can stay if you want to," Lennox says, "and deal with them." He points to where we have come from.

Lennox shows us to a place in the barbed wire where there is a tunnel dug underneath the fence. Someone before us has cut a way through the barbed wire.

"Follow me and do as I say," he says, taking off his shirt, rolling it up tightly, and stuffing it down the front of his pants.

"This is no time to be shy," I say quietly to Innocent. "We're all taking off our shirts. It will be easier to get through." I help him undo his buttons and then wrap up his shirt into a ball. He stuffs it down the front of his trousers.

We are on our hands and knees, crawling under the fence and through a row of barbed wire. I nick myself on the wire. Blood. One of the men behind me yells. I'm not the only one bitten by the barbed wire.

"Keep moving!" says Lennox.

"Deo?" calls Innocent. "Are you there?"

"I'm right behind you. Keep crawling. Don't look back. Slowly," I say, as the barbed wire bites my brother. "Keep as close to the ground as you can."

One by one we crawl through to the other side. Lennox holds back the wire until all of us are through. Sweat is running down his face. He takes out his shirt and quickly puts it back on. We all do the same. The man who helped Innocent in the river has not come through the barbed wire. All we have now is Lennox.

"Now we run. There are animals here. Hyenas, wild dogs, buffalo, elephants, but the worst of all are the lions. We will run in a line. We must hold hands where we can. You might see some bad things. But you do not stop. If you stop running, I will leave you behind."

I look around frantically. I see no animals. The bush looks peaceful. But from the frown on Lennox's face and the worry in his eyes, I know we have reached a point of great danger. The two men look anxiously around the bush, and I can smell fear again, just like I did in Gutu.

"What about Patson? He can't run," Innocent says.

"I will carry him," says Patson's father.

The sun rises above the distant trees in the Zimbabwe that we have left behind. The morning air in South Africa is buzzing with cicadas and the business of birds. The sky above is its usual cloudless blue. It will be hot today. The bush of the park is filled with shades of green, and now that I look more closely, I can see some bucks in the distance, grazing peacefully, unaware of our presence. But there is no time to enjoy any of this.

"Let's go," says Lennox.

Now is the time for running.

13

THE PARK

We run. We stay close together.

Patson's father carries his son on his back and runs closely behind Lennox. Innocent holds on to the end of the crutch that Patson carries in his right hand. I hold Innocent's hand. We struggle to keep up. The two other men run slightly behind me. We run through an open grassland, past a herd of impalas bounding away at the sight of this human train.

On the slopes of a distant hill, several zebras look up at the unusual sound of running feet. Giraffes lazily follow our progress. They look like ships of the bush, their long necks gliding above the tops of the thorn trees. A couple of younger giraffes start following us, curious about this line of running men. Soon they pause, watch us leave, and with a twitch of their heads, return to nibbling leaves from the trees. I have never been this close to so many wild animals, but now is not the time for animal-spotting.

Ahead of me Innocent is breathing heavily, but he is

keeping up with Lennox. I wish we had the sneakers Captain Washington gave us. My feet sting from the thorns and sharp stones. There is no time to stop and pull out the thorns. Mai Maria got a good deal from us.

We run.

We run without stopping, until Lennox raises his hand. A herd of black buffalo are grazing on open grassland. The black beasts do not see us. They graze lazily, their enormous jaws moving from side to side, their tails swishing flies away. Everything looks peaceful, but Lennox has heard something. We crouch down in the long grass. I am happy for the rest.

"I'm tired, Deo," says Innocent, panting.

"We're almost there," I say, without knowing if this is true.

Patson crouches next to his father, who lies flat out on the ground. I'm not sure he will be able to get back on his feet.

"Hyena!" shouts one of the men.

We spring to our feet and look behind us. A hyena is following us. The animal is twice the size of the largest dog I've ever seen. He runs sideways, lifting his nose in the air, sniffing, and then dropping his head down onto the ground. The animal is following our trail. Lennox moves quickly to the back of the line. He turns one of the men around. His shirt is drenched with blood. He must have scratched himself quite badly going through the barbed wire. He has been bleeding all this time, his blood marking a trail behind us.

"The hyena has smelled your blood," says Lennox angrily. "Why didn't you tell me you were bleeding?"

Lennox tears the shirt off the man's back and makes it into a bandage. He wraps the cloth tightly around the man's chest. The man looks terrified as the hyena draws closer, his nose in the air sniffing the fresh blood.

"Everyone lift your bags up in the air!" shouts Lennox. "Follow me."

I watch, amazed, as Lennox lifts his bag into the air and runs directly at the oncoming hyena.

"Come on!" he shouts. "It's the only way. Hyenas are scared of things higher than them."

Innocent is stuck to the spot. There is no way that I will get him to run at a charging hyena. Patson's father cannot run with Patson on his back. I can't believe what I am about to do, but without thinking, I grab Patson's crutch.

"Innocent, Operation Look After Patson, Operation Don't Move. Okay?"

He nods. "I'll look after Patson," he says.

I turn and run after Lennox, who is running at the hyena, screaming as loudly as he can. He runs with his bag held high above his head. The two men do exactly the same. I follow them waving the crutch in the air, shouting.

But then Lennox stumbles, falls, disappears headfirst into the long grass. The two men stop, uncertain what to do now. The hyena bounds forward, growling, snapping its jaws. But just as the men are about to turn and run, the sound of a shrill whistle comes.

I know what it is before I see it: a referee's whistle.

Innocent runs past me, blowing a whistle and shaking his Bix-box high above his head. I follow him, yelling at the hyena and waving Patson's crutch over my head. The men stare as Innocent runs past them, and Lennox gets up and screams at them, "Come on! Run!"

We charge after Innocent, shouting and yelling.

It works. The hyena dips its tail between its legs and lopes away in fright. Lennox catches up with us, stops, and picks up some stones. He throws them after the hyena. I do the same, but the animal is now a long way off. Innocent gives a few more blasts from his whistle.

"You can stop now!" I shout.

My brother is trembling as he takes the whistle out of his mouth and grins at me.

"Operation Scare Hyena, Deo. We chased him off!" he says, his eyes shining. As crazy as it sounds, I think my brother is having fun.

"Where did you get that from?" I ask.

"My Bix-box," he says with a sly smile. "You don't know what I've got in here." He opens the box and pulls out a piece of string, which he ties to the whistle and slips around his neck. "Just in case," he says.

Lennox laughs. "Your brother's taught me something today," he says as we walk to where Patson and his father wait. "Next time, I'll come with a whistle."

Lennox takes the remains of the man's shirt and fixes it to a thorn tree. The blood-soaked cloth flutters in the breeze.

"This will keep the hyena busy for a while. Now we must run. We still have far to go."

Patson climbs onto his father's back, and we are off again, running. Down through the plain, past the grazing black buffalo who raise their enormous heads to stare at us, past a herd of elephants feeding on the leaves of thorn trees, through a small river where hippos lie in a deep pool, their noses and eyes and funny small ears the only signs of their huge bodies.

The two men collapse onto their knees, drink greedily from the river, splashing their faces over and over with water.

"Not too fast," warns Lennox. "It will be painful to carry so much water inside you. We are not through the park yet."

The water tastes of mud, but at least it's wet. I drink only a little and wash the sweat off my face. I sink my feet into the mud by the side of the river, grateful for the coolness. Then, just above the water line across the river, I see a stack of white bones and a skull. I walk through the shallow water, crouch down, and look at what lies bleached white and clean in the sun.

"What is it?" asks Patson.

"I don't know," I say, glancing up at Lennox, who has been watching me.

"Probably a baboon, or even a monkey," he says quickly. "Leave them. We cannot stop here."

I don't believe him. I notice the glance shared between the two men. We all know what these bones are, and they did not belong to a baboon or a monkey.

We run now with new energy.

Even Patson's father picks up his pace, and soon we leave the river behind with its grim reminder of where we are and where we might end up.

The sun moves steadily across the sky; the morning becomes hotter, giving way to midday. It feels like we have been running for hours; like the crossing of the Limpopo was a week ago. Soon the water I drank at the river starts speaking to me. The pain in my side almost makes me fall down. I notice the men behind me are moving slower. Both of them are in great pain. One of them cries out for Lennox to stop. They drank too much at the river, and now they suffer for it.

Lennox picks up a tiny pebble. "Put this under your tongue, suck on it. It will help."

I suck on a pebble as well, and it brings some relief, but nothing can stop the pains shooting up my leg. We are getting tired. Even Lennox is jogging slowly now. Patson has climbed off his father's back and is hopping and being dragged between his father and Innocent.

Lennox is worried. He keeps looking back at us, encouraging us, shouting for us to keep running. The two men run alongside him.

"We should leave them here," says one of them. "They are slowing us down. Why should we be in danger because of them?"

"We stay together," replies Lennox. "Would you want me to leave you alone in the park?"

And the conversation is over.

We run on.

Stumble on, more like it.

I can't feel anything anymore, only the sound of my heart thudding in my ears. I ignore the pain in my side, the cuts on my feet, the sweat dripping down my face. All I do is breathe in and breathe out. Put one foot in front of the other, keep a steady rhythm. My feet and legs are screaming at my brain, my lungs are begging for more air, my heart is beating double-quick time, but my brain ignores it all.

Keep running, it says. Running will bring you to safety. Keep running.

Patson is once again on his father's back. Innocent and I run on either side of him, trying to bear some of his weight. Patson's father will not give up. I see it in his eyes. They have glazed over; they see nothing. Patson weeps in frustration. He knows we are moving slowly because of him.

"Leave me, Daddy, leave me," he whispers, but Patson's father ignores his son. He runs on, gripping his son's leg more tightly around his body.

We reach the top of a rise and look down over yet another grass plain. In the distance, I see the thin line of a fence.

"The end of the park," says Lennox.

We are almost there. Then I see something lying on the ground that makes me stop.

"Lennox! Look!" I shout, pointing at what I have spotted but not wanting to believe what I have seen.

"Don't look!" shouts Lennox. He has seen it too. "Do not look. Run."

But I have looked. My brain takes a while before it understands what I have seen. I have seen the legs of a person but not the body.

But before my brain can fully understand this, I hear a sound that stops my heart, a sound that stops my breathing, a sound that crawls into my stomach and makes all the pain of running disappear. It is the most terrifying sound I have ever heard.

How can the sound be so close when we cannot see the animal that makes the terrible noise?

The sound splits me in half—I want to scream, but I am too scared to open my mouth.

"Lion!" says Lennox, looking wildly about him.

Now I know what it is to be terrified.

Innocent's trousers darken; the smell of piss. The two men behind me moan. The roar of the lion has turned us into statues. We see nothing; we hear only lion.

"Listen. Listen carefully." This is Lennox whispering. He is looking all around, trying to find where the sound is coming from. "Nobody must run. If you run away, it is over."

His voice is low but firm, something to hold on to.

"Listen to Lennox," I manage to whisper to Innocent, who looks all around him, confused by the size of the sound that has covered us all.

"We must hold hands. Walk slowly away. Toward the fence." Lennox is very afraid, but he is concentrating.

I understand what he wants. If one of us runs away, the lion has something to spring upon. If we stay together we might have a chance. The others seem to understand. Out here we stand no chance alone. We once again grab one another's hands. We form a line. We move slowly away from the sound. There might be more than one lion.

Lennox leads us down the rise, away from the sound of lions feeding. Now my legs want to fly, now my heart is pumping, now everything is screaming to my brain, Run for your life.

But we walk.

Now we walk faster. Now we jog. Now Lennox allows us to run. He sweeps Patson off his father's back, throws me his bag, and hoists Patson over his shoulder and runs.

The fence gets nearer, the sound of the lions fading behind us. Patson's father, free from the burden of his son, runs. Innocent holds on to my hand and we run together, as fast as the wind, our legs pumping, our bodies flying through the grass.

The two men run ahead, faster than us. They are the first to reach the fence. They start climbing.

"No!" shouts Lennox.

Too late. The wire fizzes, crackles, and the men shriek and fall to the ground as the electricity burns them.

"Not there—I'll show you," says Lennox, helping up the dazed men and leading us along the length of the fence until we get to a section that's been cut open, the wire carefully handwoven together to look as if it is whole. In a few minutes Lennox has opened the hole and we are through, out of the park.

We walk slowly, exhausted, relieved not to be running. We come to a dusty road beside the fence.

"You can wait here," says Lennox. "It is safe here. Someone will come and pick you up. You just have to wait."

The two men glance at each other. They will not wait here in the middle of nowhere. They begin jogging along the road. Patson and his father are too exhausted to go anywhere. So is Innocent. We have no choice but to wait.

"And you?" I ask Lennox.

He points back to the park. "I go back."

"Thank you. Thank you for getting us to South Africa," I say.

He nods, smiles at Innocent, and says to him, "Thank you for chasing the hyena away." Then he trots back the way we came.

We collapse at the side of the road in the middle of nowhere. I am so thirsty, my throat aches for a drink.

Sleep.

I wake to the sound of an engine.

Through the glare, I see a truck driving toward us, billowing dust behind it. Brakes squeak. The truck stops next to us.

The smell of tomatoes.

A white man leans out of his window. "You want work?"

Patson's father gets to his feet. Innocent looks up at the man, shields his eyes from the sun.

"You want to work, you get in the back of the truck, otherwise I leave you here," he says, revving the engine.

We climb in, helping Patson's father hoist Patson up. Innocent sits down on one of the boxes, and the wood cracks.

"Don't sit on the bloody boxes!" shouts the truck driver.

On the side of each box is a label — FLYING TOMATO FARM.

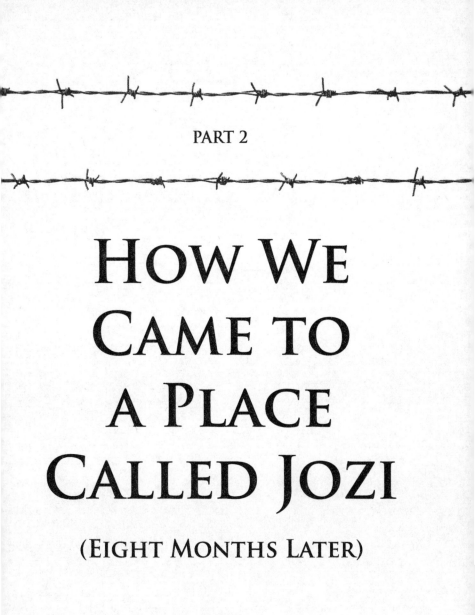

PART 2

HOW WE CAME TO A PLACE CALLED JOZI

(EIGHT MONTHS LATER)

14

FLYING TOMATO FARM

I kick an empty tin can on the road, and it sails through the air, landing with a clunk. Sunday soccer at Khomele village is over, and I cannot go back there, not after what happened. I will miss the soccer but not the angry stares of the adults.

I walk through the large gate of the Flying Tomato Farm and look up at the sign of the red tomato with angel wings that hangs over the gate. The farm is not the heaven I thought it was eight months ago when we arrived in the back of the truck.

This new thought pops and crackles in my head as I walk back to my room behind the packing shed. The words of the men at Khomele village buzz around in my mind. I didn't understand everything they said, but what I saw in their faces was clear enough. We are not wanted here.

"Deo? Why did those men shout at us?" Innocent's question comes from a long way off. I am not really listening to him. He walks beside me, dragging his feet in the dust and shaking his head from side to side. "I didn't do anything. Not to them. They shouldn't shout at me. I don't like that. You scored a goal, and I was happy. It's always like that. I fly when you score. Always."

I have no answer for him. What happened at Khomele today has started me thinking again.

When we first arrived at the Flying Tomato Farm, I had to pinch myself every morning to make sure that I wasn't dreaming. Innocent and I had beds to sleep in, with our own blankets and pillows. We had a roof over our heads, and we weren't running. We ate two meals a day, and at the end of the month we got fifty South African rands—almost seven billion Zim dollars each, just for picking tomatoes!

I had never seen such a beautiful farm in all my life. Benjamin, the twice-removed second cousin of the nephew of the Modjadji Rain Queen, laughed at how often my mouth dropped open at what I saw on the farm. He is what they call the *madala* on the farm, and he has worked here all his life. His nephew, Philani, always teased Innocent and me. He called us the "how-whe" birds because we were always gaping at everything.

The many fields of tomato bushes stretching out in straight lines toward the foot of the faraway Soutpansberg Mountains; the rows of white plastic tents covering the young bushes, protecting them from the hot Limpopo sun; the gleaming tractors and cultivating machines driving up and down the road from the packing shed to the fields; the bright fluorescent lights in the packing house and the moving conveyor belt filled with red, tumbling tomatoes, picked and packed by twenty fast-moving hands into boxes; the white men in their short pants, always busy, jumping in and out of their cars or trucks, shouting instructions in a language that sounded like they were clearing their throats all the time, always watching, always talking into their cell phones.

At first I thought we had landed in heaven and that life could never get better than this. Each morning Innocent and I got up at six o'clock to wait for the truck to take us to the tomato fields. There we would work until midmorning, preparing the soil, spraying the leaves, picking the tomatoes, and loading them into crates to be packed into the back of the truck. After eating breakfast we would work again until three o' clock and then come back to the farm to wash and sort the tomatoes. At five o'clock the bell would ring, and then we'd eat again.

I didn't pay careful enough attention to what happened to Patson and his father. I didn't want to see how the foreman would not allow Patson to work, and that meant his father couldn't stay on the farm, so they were handed over to the police. I was sorry I didn't say good-bye to Patson and his father. They were here only two days, and on the third morning I woke up and saw their beds were empty. Philani told me later that the police were waiting for them at the gate and took them away.

"And my uncle works for these men," said Philani bitterly a few days after. "He knows what is happening here, but he will not leave."

"But why would he want to leave if he has been here all his life?" I asked.

"You wait," he said. "The water from the Limpopo is still wet behind your ears. You're still fresh meat that made it out of the park. You'll see what I'm talking about."

Philani is the joker on the farm—but you never know whether he is laughing at you or with you. I think there is some trouble between him and his uncle. Benjamin is very strict with Philani and says that being eighteen doesn't make him an adult. They argue a lot. Philani doesn't want to be here; he is always talking about leaving.

My life on the Flying Tomato Farm was too busy to worry about what had happened to Patson and his father or why it was that not all the workers were happy. I didn't pay much attention to why they and Philani whispered angrily to one another late at night outside my window or why they looked at Foreman Gerber with hatred in their eyes.

In the beginning I was only too happy not to think too much. We were strangers here, and that was enough to worry about. I also had to keep an eye on Innocent and make sure that when the boss was around, he played the adult game we had worked out.

"Now it is time for Operation Innocent and Deo Are

Adults," I told him on the third night on the farm, after I noticed the foreman looking at him closely as we signed our contracts.

"I can do that," said Innocent.

And he could. None of the white foremen noticed that Innocent was different, because whenever they came near he was busy with our "operation." Except the first time we were paid and Innocent grinned at Gerber when the foreman handed him one fifty-rand note.

"Where is the rest of the money?" asked Innocent loudly. "One piece of paper isn't enough to buy my batteries."

I quickly took his money and moved him away, explaining to him that here the money was different. That was when Philani stepped in and made a joke about how we still expected to be paid in wheelbarrows of money. Everyone laughed, and the attention was drawn away from Innocent. Later, Benjamin came over to us while we were eating. For a while he didn't speak; he leaned against the wall of the packing shed, regarding my brother.

"Who's looking after whom?" he asked at last.

Innocent looked up at him, shrugged, and cleaned up the gravy on his plate with a piece of bread. Could this white-haired old man be trusted?

"We look after each other," I said carefully.

"Of course you do. Are we not all our brothers' keepers?" he said with a twinkle in his eye. I stared at him without answering, not knowing if this was some sort of trap.

"How old are you, Deo?"

"I'm seventeen," I said quickly, lying by two years.

"No, you're not," chirped in Innocent. "There are ten years between us. And I'm twenty-five. So that makes Deo fifteen, and not a day older."

I could've kicked Innocent then, but the old man laughed at my brother's face.

"You don't need to be afraid of me, Deo," he said to me. "I will tell no one about your brother. You are safe here now, but keep him out of trouble, and listen to Foreman Gerber and the others. There are a lot of places worse than the Flying Tomato Farm. If you work hard, you will do well here."

And he was right. We worked hard and stayed out of trouble, and we did well.

At first I was happy to listen to old Benjamin and stay on the farm and not go anywhere else. After all we had been through, I wanted to be in one place only. I liked getting up every morning and not worrying about where we were going or when we would next be eating or sleeping. I liked doing the same thing every day.

I suppose I was like a ghost hovering above the shell of me, watching myself spraying tomatoes, picking tomatoes, packing tomatoes, and even eating tomatoes. It was so easy not to think about what happened to Amai and Grandpa Longdrop. If I worked hard, they stayed away and I didn't have time to invite them into my mind. I didn't have to push down the lump in my throat. By nighttime, I was too tired to lie awake and think about them and what had happened to us back in Gutu. And, come Sundays, I had something else to keep me from thinking.

On Sundays I played soccer with the boys from Khomele village, right next door to the Flying Tomato Farm.

I can smell out a soccer pitch anywhere, anytime, and by the second weekend at the Flying Tomato Farm I had found out where the local boys played. One Sunday I walked across the road to Khomele village to watch. The next Sunday I returned, and the boys invited me to join them. At first I played cautiously, staying on the fringes of the game, checking out the skills of the other players.

I was always chosen last, which I didn't mind. At least I got a game. I learned quickly that these boys played very differently from what I was used to. The ball they played with allowed for a much faster game. It had more spring it its bounce than my billion-dollar ball (which didn't hold a billion dollars anymore, but sixteen pink fifty-rand notes), and I had to adjust to it bouncing quickly off my foot, making it harder to control. I learned, too, that doing tricks with the ball counted for a lot in their eyes.

And so we played each Sunday, and I became bolder, scoring a couple of goals, making some good passes, learning a few fancy tricks, and soon I was always one of the first to be chosen.

What more could I ask for? Soccer on Sundays, free food,

a place to sleep, a beautiful farm, money each month, a fading memory of Gutu, and a happy Innocent. Can you blame me if I thought I was in heaven?

But what happened at Khomele village today has started me thinking again.

I was playing soccer, and Innocent was listening to his radio on the sidelines — until I scored a goal. It had been a particularly great goal, the result of a four-pass move ending with my sizzling left foot curling the ball out of reach of the goalie. The boys on my team were congratulating me, and we were running around lifting our shirts up and shouting like they do on television. Innocent was running up the sideline, his arms outstretched, shouting *"Goooaaal!"* when he bumped into some of the adult men who had come over to watch the game. One of them grabbed him by the arm and pushed him hard.

"Get out of here, Zimbo! What are you doing in Khomele?"

I ran over and faced the group of men.

"We play here every Sunday," I said. "Why did you push my brother?"

"Because he's a lion from Zimbabwe and he comes here to eat our food," said a young man, pointing at Innocent.

"And he takes our work," said another man. He had the bloodshot eyes of someone who likes the taste of liquor.

"I know you work at the Flying Tomato Farm too. I've seen you on their trucks. You should be at school — you are too young to be doing the work of men." This from an older man, whom I had seen sitting outside one of the huts. He seemed to be one of the elders of Khomele, as the others grew quiet when he spoke.

I had nothing to say in the face of such anger. The men stared at us with such hatred that it took my breath away.

"What do you get paid each month?" asked the man with bloodshot eyes.

"Fifty rand," I answered, backing away.

"We cannot live for fifty rand a month, but you hungry lions don't know what real money is," said the younger man bitterly. "You are happy with little because you don't know any better."

"Deo, let's go," said Innocent from behind me.

"Get out of here!" shouted the elder of Khomele, and then he turned to the boys of the village who were standing watching. "If these two come back to Khomele, there will be no more soccer. We don't want *kwerekwere* here!"

"You come back and you'll feel some of this," the younger man said to Innocent, shaking his fist. Innocent backed away hurriedly, lifting his hands in apology. The boys on the pitch turned away from me. One of them picked up the soccer ball and walked away. The game was over. I would not be back next Sunday.

Kwerekwere.

I had never heard that word before.

As I walked out of Khomele, I looked around at the small

village with new eyes. This place was very different from the Flying Tomato Farm. The windmill was broken, the houses were not painted, and the land was not cultivated. Here there were no tractors turning the soil; instead the men used hand plows. While everything hummed with activity across the road, here there was no action. The men sat around in front of their huts; only the women were busy with domestic chores. Here there were no conveyor belts, fluorescent lights, roof-high boxes of vegetables. Was there not enough work for these men on the Flying Tomato Farm? Surely earning fifty rand a month is better than earning nothing?

And this word *kwerekwere* — what did it mean?

15

PHILANI'S DEAL

The Flying Tomato Farm is Sunday-quiet.

The packing shed is deserted. The roads are empty of vehicles. There is no one in the fields. We have come back earlier than usual. There is nothing to do, so I go to my bed in the corner of the room and take out the leather pouch from under my pillow. My soccer ball is now pancake-flat.

Innocent goes to the basin and washes his hands. He scrubs his fingernails, the palms of his hands. After drying his hands, he takes out his Bix-box, which he has stuffed under the foot of his mattress. He knows that I have started thinking again and watches me silently.

Meanwhile, I unpick the thread and take out the sixteen fifty-rand notes. I lay each note on my pillow.

"That's a lot of money you've got lying around. You'd better look after it—there are greedy eyes on this farm."

Philani is leaning against the open door and staring at the money. I scoop up the money and stuff it under my pillow.

"I heard what happened at Khomele today," he says, walking into my room. He slumps on the foot of my bed, winks at Innocent, and leans back against the wall. "Looks like you'll have to find another soccer game. There's a pitch about five miles from here, over the hills, but it's a long way to walk for a game."

"I don't need to play with them," I say stupidly.

He nods. "They might hurt your brother."

"I didn't do anything to them. They shouldn't shout at me. It's not Innocent's fault. Not one bit," says Innocent sadly.

I have nothing to say to Philani, but he is right. They have threatened Innocent, and I will not go there again.

"Why do they hate us?" asks Innocent.

"You took their jobs, Innocent. Before the people started coming across the river from Zimbabwe, the men from Khomele village worked on the Flying Tomato Farm. In those days Foreman Gerber paid them four hundred rand a month."

"Is that a lot of money?" asks Innocent.

"Then your people started coming out of the park and ate Gerber's tomatoes. He caught them and handed them over to the police, and the police sent them back across the border. But then Gerber got an idea. He would catch them, bring them here, and give them two choices: work for him or be arrested by the police.

"When you come to a new land, you don't know how things work. You have no friends, no family to help you. Who would not take food, a place to sleep, and work if it was offered?"

"They called us *kwerekwere*. What does that mean?" I ask.

"Foreigner. Outsider. One who does not belong."

So this is what I am — a foreigner in this land. I have come from outside and I do not belong. I never knew there was a word for this.

"You are not alone, Deo. There are thousands of people who come to find work in South Africa. And it is hard for the men from Khomele. They lose their jobs, and then they see people from across the river eating the food they used to eat and getting the money they used to get. They're very angry, and who can blame them?"

"I would be angry too," I say. "But then why are the men who work here also unhappy?"

"Ah, that's easy to explain. It is because they have no choice. They have become slaves of the Flying Tomato Farm, Deo. If they complain about the pay, Gerber will hand them over to the South African police. The police will lock them up in their van and send them back across the river. None of them wants to go back, and so everyone keeps quiet. They work and get paid very little, while the men at Khomele do not work and do not get paid."

"And Foreman Gerber can pay what he wants," I say, understanding for the first time why the men whispered angrily in the middle of the night. "Fifty cents even, and we would be so grateful."

"Life in Jozi is better than working in this dump. I have a friend in Jozi who fixes motorcars. When I worked in Jozi, he paid me a thousand rand a month."

"A thousand rand a month! That's a fortune."

He laughs at me. "Yes, it is. And if I ask him, he will give you and your brother work too. I have a place to stay — you could stay with me for a while until you find your own place." Philani speaks so softly and quickly, it's easy to believe him. "In Jozi there are things that you have never seen before. It's much better than being stuck out here. I will take you there, but you will need to pay for my taxi. Once we get work, I'll pay you back. My uncle doesn't allow me any money."

So now the truth comes. Philani has no money, and so he cannot leave the Flying Tomato Farm. This is Philani's deal. He takes us to Jozi and gets us work and a place to stay in exchange for me paying for his taxi fare. It seems a fair deal.

"How much is the taxi ride?" I ask.

"One-way from Musina to the Jozi train station is one hundred rand."

I quickly do the math: three hundred rand for transport for the three of us leaves Innocent and me another five hundred rand to live on. Five hundred is so many billion Zim dollars that we shouldn't have any trouble living off that for at least six months.

Innocent takes out his photograph from his Bix-box. "Zero-two-one-six-five-eight-three-two-one-four," he says quietly.

"Okay, so are you going to tell me what that number is, Innocent?"

"Zero-two-one-six-five-eight-three-two-one-four," he says, grinning at me, happy to have distracted me from my conversation with Philani.

"Yes. So?"

"Where he's at," he says, pointing at the photograph. "The telephone number on the Removals truck. Dad's work. We still going to find him, Deo? Right?" He leans over and hands me the photograph.

I've never thought about finding my father in the same way that Innocent does. If he wanted to see us, he would have come back to Gutu a long time ago. But what if, by some miracle, we could find him in South Africa? What if he was pleased to see us? Perhaps we could stay with him? Perhaps he has a house? I know how to look after Innocent; he wouldn't have to worry about him. We don't need much money to survive, and I could go to school again, and we could be together. I look at my father in Innocent's photograph. The man looks happy enough to be with his Zimbabwean family....

"It is time to leave this place," I say, making a decision that was waiting in the shadows for me to find it.

"Good. It's the right decision. We must get to Musina and catch a taxi to Jozi. If you hang around here the police will find you, arrest you, and send you back. You must go to the city."

Johannesburg. Jozi. I have heard about this place. Everyone talks about going to Jozi: plenty of work, plenty of money.

We didn't leave Gutu, flee from the Green Bombas, cross the Limpopo River, escape from the Ghuma-ghuma, and run through the park to end up in this place.

"Will you help us go to Jozi, Philani?"

16

JOZI

Innocent, Philani, and me—flying in a taxi—stuffed between thirteen other men and women going to Johannesburg.

When we stop in the town of Musina, Philani takes us to a two-for-the-price-of-one PEP store with nice, nice clothes.

"If we're going to Jozi, we've got to look sharp. It's time to throw these clothes away and buy what you like," he says as we wander through the shop, dazed at the quality and variety of the clothes.

"We get one free?" asks Innocent, holding up a T-shirt.

"That's how it works here, boys. Two for the price of one rules!"

We buy new shirts, jeans, shoes. I throw away my old clothes right there and then. Philani laughs at us and rolls his eyes at the shop person as we go in and out of the changing room with piles of clothes.

"Now you boys are ready for Jozi," he says as we leave the shop, swinging our bags of clothes.

*   *   *

The Soutpansberg Mountains are forgotten; the rows of red tomatoes forgotten; the boys of Khomele village forgotten. Philani does all the talking as the countryside whizzes past. All we do is stare at things I could never have imagined: wide, wide roads with five lanes packed with so many shiny, smart cars. Roads built in the sky with lights. Long two-lane tunnels right through a mountain.

At the next stop, a place called Louis Trichardt, Philani takes us into a clean, clean shop with loud music where every shelf is packed with sweets, chocolates, nuts, chewing gum. Big loaves of white bread twice the size we get in Zimbabwe. We gawk at the women who drink beer, smoke cigarettes, talk as loudly as men, and wear modern clothes that no woman from Gutu would wear.

"In South Africa anything is possible. You can be poor one day, and a multimillionaire the next day. Look. Saturday's lotto draw is ten million rand! Ten million rand!" he says and shows us how to play.

And it's true. The board says I can win ten million rand on Saturday. I can't even do the math as to how many gazillions of dollars that would be in Zimbabwe.

"Choose six numbers, Innocent, and you can be a millionaire. Fill in the square, pay twenty rand, and we wait for the draw on Saturday night. You've got *lucky* rubbed on your forehead. I can see it.

"Give me another twenty rand, Deo, and you can play too. Hey, maybe all three of us should play? That gives us three chances of winning. Give me another twenty rand, and I'll also try. I'll keep all the tickets for us. If one of us has the lucky number we all share. Cool? Cool."

And that's Philani's new deal. It sounds like he knows what he is doing. So I give him sixty rand, choose my numbers, and watch how they are entered into a machine.

"We're going to be millionaires this weekend," he says, kissing the tickets and stuffing them into his pocket.

Sounds like a good deal to me.

In Mokopane Philani shows us how to order finger-licking chicken and Fanta Grape. "Order whatever you want, Innocent. Look at those pictures—doesn't it make your stomach grumble? A streetwise deal gets you two chicken pieces, chips, and a cool drink. What do you want, Deo?"

I can't believe how easy it is. The photos seem so real, you can almost taste the food. Behind the counter men and women in smart uniforms are busy cooking, packing, and selling. People are lining up and giving orders, and moments later they walk out of the shop with brown paper bags of chicken and fries. It's all so quick, so easy. Philani calls it "fast food," and I can see why.

"That will be forty-four rand, Deo. Give me that fifty-rand note—that will be enough. You don't need the silver change—

those coins aren't worth much. What a bargain, hey? This is much better than tomatoes on the farm."

And Philani is right. The food is delicious. I've never tasted anything so good. Innocent grins as he licks his fingers.

"It's like the sign says, finger-licking good. Can I have some more, Deo?"

And I buy three more boxes of streetwise chicken, the best meal I have ever had.

After hours and hours on the road, my stomach full and my eyes tired from seeing so much, I fall asleep in the taxi. Innocent leans against the window and snores quietly, his Bix-box lying loosely in his lap. I rest my head against his shoulder, and soon I am dreaming.

I wake up only for a moment as the taxi goes over a bump in the road, and I see a sign flash by: WARMBATHS 10 KM.

Warmbaths. Sounds like a nice place. I wouldn't mind a warm bath. As I start to drift off to sleep again, I overhear the people behind me talking quietly.

"We can't do business with these people, because today he calls himself Abdul, and tomorrow he is Muhammed."

"I know what you mean. The Somalis are Arabs and Muslims, and those countries have lots of money, and they help only their countrymen."

"While our own country does nothing to help us."

"They should put those Somalis in camps and send them back."

"These refugees are causing too much trouble."

"Too much trouble."

My dreams take over, and I am far away again.

I wake up to shiny, tall glass buildings piercing the sky.

And lights—a blinking, dazzling, never-ending stream of lights—so many lights it makes my head dizzy. We tumble out of the taxi and look around at the night, which is almost as bright as day. Thick, big buildings have eaten up all the trees and grass, and the thousands of people are talking, shouting, moving in every direction.

Jozi.

I don't know where to look first. The city is all around me, noisy, sparkling, and overwhelming. Next to the Nelson Mandela Bridge there is a giant soccer ball—the largest soccer ball I have ever seen.

"What's that?" I ask Philani.

"You don't know about the soccer World Cup? All the nations of the world will come here to play."

Of course I knew about the World Cup, but not that it was happening here, in South Africa!

Innocent is holding my hand tightly and has the index finger of his left hand pressed into his ear.

"There is a storm coming, Deo," he says, shaking his head as if there is an insect crawling around inside. "There's a storm coming. I can feel it."

Innocent does this sometimes. He feels the weather change.

He can tell us about a storm days before it arrives. Grandpa Longdrop said that Innocent was our own weather satellite, and he was more trustworthy than any radio weather reports. He walks around now with his fingers in his ears, looking miserable.

"Stay close to me," I whisper to him. "Philani will take us to his home. Don't worry about the storm."

There is something wrong with Philani. He is irritated. He is not so talkative now and glances back at us as we follow him to the next taxi stand.

"We need to take another taxi to Alexandra," he says, holding his hand out for more money. I am too tired to ask any questions, so I hand him some notes.

We climb into another taxi. Now no one talks as we speed through the night. This driver seems to be in a great hurry. He doesn't stop at the red lights, and the other passengers in our taxi shout at him and he shouts back. He blasts the horn and flashes his lights at cars in his way. He seems angry and overtakes on corners. I close my eyes, not wanting to see the big truck crash into us. The passengers shout at him. He doesn't answer them but just goes faster.

Innocent is in the back corner with his eyes closed and both his fingers pressed into his ears.

"What's wrong with your brother?" asks Philani when we get out of the taxi and walk along the dark streets of Alexandra.

"Nothing. I think he's a little scared. He'll be okay," I say, staring at the crush of shacks and huts, packed closely to one another. We have left the road and walk down narrow alley-ways, following Philani through the heart of this township called Alexandra. He walks fast. Every so often he turns around to check that we are still following him.

A gunshot makes me jump. Screams and angry voices follow.

"Come on," says Philani, and he starts running. It's hard to keep up. It's almost like he's running away from us. The doors of the shacks are closed; curious faces appear in the windows.

Philani is more than irritated. He is upset, almost angry. He stops before a small shack stuffed between two other huts at the end of a pathway. Inside is light, and people are moving about. He looks at us nervously and then looks back at the hut.

"Wait here," he commands and calls to someone. The door is opened by a man who stares briefly at Philani before slapping him across the face. It happens so suddenly that I'm not even sure I saw it. Philani is crying now, holding his cheek and backing away. He points to us and talks in a rush of a language I do not understand. The man comes out of the house to glare at us.

This is not going well. Innocent slips behind me and searches for my hand. The man looks very unhappy. I don't like the look of him at all.

"Come here," he says, and I step forward. Will he slap me too?

"Philani says you paid for him to come back from Musina. Is that right?"

I nod. Philani has disappeared into the hut, and there is a lot of noise of "look who's here" and "Philani's back" coming from inside.

"He says you need a place to sleep for one night?"

"I thought that..." I do not finish.

"You can sleep at the back here, but tomorrow when I wake up, you're gone. We don't want any refugees here. Understand?"

I nod again. What can I say to this big, angry man? I want to speak to Philani, but he's inside. The man takes us around to the back. He unlocks a small shed and turns on the light. The shed is packed with parts of cars, old batteries, and exhaust pipes. Tires are stacked in a pile in one corner.

"Don't touch anything, or I'll beat the crap out of you" is all the man says before he closes the door. I hear him lock the padlock. We are prisoners in his shed.

Innocent looks very upset, like he's going to cry. His finger is pressed deeply into his right ear.

"I want to go back to the Flying Tomato Farm, Deo. Why are we here?" he says.

I cannot bear the accusation in his voice.

"Do you think I planned this?" I ask. "Do you think this is what I expected? Philani said that we would be given a place to sleep. I didn't know it would be on the floor of a garage."

I kick angrily at a tire that is lying around.

"But where are we going to sleep, Deo? At the Flying Tomato Farm..."

"We are not at the farm anymore, Innocent. We are here in Jozi."

Innocent looks up at me for the first time. "But I don't like this place, Deo. It's not very friendly. The people speak a different language. They look at me funny."

"Because you *are* funny!" I shout at him. "You walk around with your fingers in your ears, holding on to your stupid cereal box. Talking like a baby. Don't you see? That's why people look at you. You're funny to look at, funny boy!"

The words come out harder than rocks, sharper than nails. Innocent dips his head as if he is being beaten. He doesn't look at me but shakes his head and walks quickly to the far corner of the shed. He stumbles over some junk and falls to the ground. He drops his Bix-box and some of his treasure falls out.

I want to help him up, but I don't.

With one finger still pressed into his ear, he picks up his stuff and carefully puts everything back into his tin box.

He's sobbing. "It's not Innocent's fault. The doctor is the one you must speak to. It's not my fault he went to sleep," he says, gulping air between sobs.

He closes the lid of his Bix-box and walks to the pile of tires, where he sits down with his back to me. "The doctor made a mistake. It's his fault. Not Innocent. Shouting at me is not right. Amai does not like that. Grandpa Longdrop will be angry with you when I tell him. I didn't do anything to you."

I hold back the scream of anger. I shouted at Innocent because of how people looked at *me*.

I was scared when we arrived in Jozi, scared in the taxi, scared when we ran through the township to Philani's home, scared of the man in the doorway who slapped Philani. I am scared now, so I shouted at Innocent.

Suddenly, I'm so tired. I want to sleep. I pull tires from the pile and arrange them into some sort of bed. I stuff clothes into my soccer pouch to make a pillow. Innocent ignores me. I lie down on the tires, arrange my soccer-pillow behind my head, and stare up at the ceiling. "Zero-two-one-eight-five-six-one-two-four-two," I say quietly. "No, that's not right." I say another string of numbers to myself. "No, that's not right either. How can I be so stupid to forget such an important number?" I speak out loud another series of numbers and glance over at Innocent. I know he is listening. "It's no good. I just don't have the brains for this. How am I supposed to find Dad if I can't even remember his number? I'm stupid. If only I had remembered to write it down. If only I had a brain clever enough to remember numbers. Now I'm never going to be able to phone him. If only I could remember the number," I say, telling myself off.

"Zero-two-one-six-five-eight-three-two-one-four,"

says Innocent quietly. "It's not difficult, Deo. You just have to let the numbers talk to you. They organize themselves in your head. You shouldn't try so hard."

"Okay, come and lie here next to me and tell me how you do it," I say.

He gets up and comes over next to me.

Innocent repeats the phone number of our father's work. "Now you say it and try and listen to the numbers."

I repeat the correct number slowly.

"You see, you're not dumb, Deo."

"Thank you, Innocent. And you're not funny either."

"I know that. But you are," he says, and I hear a joke creeping into his voice. "We have a place that gives us food and a bed and money every month, but my little brother doesn't want that place. That's funny."

"You're right, Innocent," I say, laughing. "I'm the one who's funny. Not you."

"Okay. You're the funny boy, not me. No, not Innocent."

Innocent is happy now, my angry words forgotten. And we go to sleep, with peace between us, until we are woken in the morning by the sound of the door being unlocked and a gruff, unfriendly voice telling us to get our things, leave, and never come back.

17

ALEXANDRA TOWNSHIP

The storm came seven days later.

We try to keep dry, but there's nowhere to escape from raindrops the size of pebbles. In the end we join some people from Mozambique and Somaliland who have made a fire under a bridge. All around us the storm lights the sky, and we huddle next to the blazing fire. I have never seen such lightning or heard such thunder. The rain pours down as if a dam has opened in the sky. Innocent cowers in a corner under the bridge, both his fingers in his ears. He is too scared to worry about sitting around the fire. It's best to let him wait out the storm in the only way he knows how.

I stand close to the fire, stomping my feet and stretching my hands out in front of me, listening to the men. They talk about a letter that has been sent to some of their friends.

"We should go to the police!" one of them says angrily.

"Don't be stupid. They won't help us."

"But they cannot tell us to close our shops. Who is the writer of this letter?"

"It gives no name of a person and is signed the Alexandra Retailers' Association."

"Close our shops, but this is not right!"

"This is bad, very bad. Listen to what it says: 'The business, political, and community leadership of Alexandra is currently engaged in finding a solution for the influx of your shops into our communities.' "

The man stops only because everyone is speaking at once. I've never heard the word *influx*. Sounds like a disease.

"Let him finish," one of them says, pointing to the man holding the letter.

He continues to read. " 'All matters regarding your existence in our communities are being discussed. We've had engagement with all relevant stakeholders, and our cries are still heard only by the deaf, and therefore we have taken it upon ourselves to resolve this matter.' "

"And we know what that means!"

But I do not know what any of this means. The men continue to talk, and I tune them out. Instead, I lose myself in the colors of the warm flames and forget that I am wet and hungry. The last seven days on the streets of Alexandra have been hard. We sleep where we can, eat what we find, drink water from the community tap. And every night that we sleep out in the open, I think how stupid I was to leave the Flying Tomato Farm.

Sunday has come and gone, and we are still not million-aires. I tried to find Philani to ask him what has happened to our lotto tickets, but the man at his house said that Philani was not living there anymore and that we should go back to where we came from.

We are not wanted in Alexandra. Wherever we turn, people scowl at us, saying things like, "There is no place for you here. Go back home."

I'm getting used to being chased away in Jozi. If it's not the people in Alexandra, then it's the security guards, and if it's not the security guards, then it's the police. You don't want to be caught by the police. I've seen them tumble people into the back of their vans and drive away. I make sure that we always run a mile when we see the men in blue uniforms.

All week now we have walked through the township looking for a place to sleep, and all the time we are running out of money. Things are very expensive here. The money I brought with us from the Flying Tomato Farm is gone.

The people in Alexandra are poor. Their homes are not homes but shacks put together with sheets of plastic, sign-boards, pieces of wood, and wire netting. There is no place to go to the toilet. There is nowhere for Innocent to wash his hands, and this is making him crazy.

Finally, the storm has passed. It has stopped raining. The men have drifted away. I have no idea how long I have been sitting next to a dying fire. I look up and see that Innocent has disappeared.

The fear of losing him here, in angry Jozi, is the worst fear I've felt so far. But there is nowhere he could have gone.

"Innocent!"

A few of the men who are walking away shrug when I shout at them, asking if they've seen my brother. On the highway the cars speed past, the spray from their tires floating on the air.

Now I am alone under the bridge and furious.

I run up the side of the bridge and look up and down the road crossing the highway.

No sign of Innocent.

How many times have I told him never to go anywhere without me? If he wanders off by himself, I will never find him!

I dodge through the traffic and run across the bridge and then run down to look around at the base on the other side of the highway.

Nothing.

Now I am really scared. What do I do?

"Where are you, Innocent?" I say aloud, just to hear a voice. I charge back up the side of the bridge, cross the highway, and run back to where I left him curled up against one of the cement pillars.

"Are you looking for your brother?" asks a voice.

I can't see anyone.

"Up here!"

I look up. A face looks downward at me through a hole in

the bridge. The man is wearing a black stocking covering his hair and a leopard-print shirt.

"You looking for your brother?" he asks again from his upside-down position.

I stare up at the man in the hole in the roof of the bridge. "Yes. His name's Innocent."

"I know his name. You must be Deo, right?"

"Yes. Where's Innocent?"

"Here, give me your hand."

He offers me his hand. I pull myself up and climb through the hole. Once inside, I scramble to my feet into a world that is dark and quiet. I see sheets glowing with golden light and the shadows of people's heads. I hear the laughter of little children.

"Come this way. You'll get used to the dark," says the man, holding my hand lightly and leading me deeper inside the bridge.

There, behind one of the sheets, I recognize the silhouette of my brother. Innocent is sitting on a bed, playing cards with two children. On a small table is a paraffin lamp burning brightly. A sheet has been fixed to the top of the cement ceiling, creating a screen. I see more silhouettes on the other side of another sheet.

"Welcome, Deo. We've heard a lot about you," says the man with the black stocking on his head. "My name is Gawalia. I like your brother — he is good with my children."

A man and a woman look around the sheet that separates them from Innocent and the children. The man lifts his hand in silent greeting. Farther down, another woman appears out of the gloom. She stands with her hands on her hips and shakes her head from side to side at the sight of me. She is a beautiful woman: long, braided hair; silver earrings dangling from her ears; lips red with lipstick; and toothpaste-white teeth.

"Gawalia, why must you pick up every stray dog in Jozi that comes under our bridge?" she asks with laughter in her voice.

"I picked you up, Angel," says Gawalia, waving her away. "You were a stray kitten, and look what a cat you turned out to be!"

Now that my eyes have adjusted to the strange light I can see more clearly. The empty concrete space inside the bridge has been transformed into people's homes. Against one wall is a kitchen table covered with sauces and spices. There are three deck chairs, and behind each curtained partition I can make out beds. In the background, there is the constant sound of cars driving through rainwater. It's a soft, shushing sound, strangely comforting.

"Tsepo and Rasta are very good at cards, Deo. They always win," says Innocent, grinning at me as if he had never left my side.

"Hello, Innocent's brother," says one of the children.

"Come on, Tsepo, deal!" says Rasta.

I am quickly forgotten as they collect their cards, sort them out, and look at the hands they have been dealt.

"It was quite a storm out there. Are you hungry, Deo?" asks Gawalia.

I have no words. All I want to do is to cry at his softly spoken question. The last person who asked me if I was hungry was Amai. I nod gratefully as he gestures for me to sit at the kitchen table.

"Here, try some of what was left over from last night." He scrapes out some rice, with flecks of meat and vegetables, into a metal plate. "Innocent tells me that you have come from Masvingo Province."

I look up in amazement, my mouth full of the delicious food.

"I'm from Gweru. It's not far from Bikita." Does this man know about Commander Jesus too?

I nod toward Tsepo and Rasta playing with Innocent.

"Their mother is dead" is all Gawalia says at my unasked question. "They like Innocent. They found him crying outside and so invited him to come up. They haven't done that to anyone since their mother died."

The man and woman step out from behind their sheet and join us at the table.

"Ah, our two lovebirds. This is Catarina Manungo, and this is Rais Sewika. She is from Mozambique, and he is from the Democratic Republic of Congo. They want to get married," says Gawalia, stoking up a paraffin burner to boil water. "And this is Deo. He is from my homeland."

Rais greets me while Catarina moves over to the bed where Innocent and the children play.

"Is he what you are looking for, Gawalia?" asks Catarina.

"He could be," answers Gawalia, waving his hand in the air as if he doesn't want to discuss the subject.

"I would ask him," says Rais. "We can't do it anymore, Gawalia. We've got our own things to do."

Gawalia sighs. "Rais is in a band. He plays at night and works during the day. Catarina is a waitress and brings home lots of leftovers," explains Gawalia, pointing at my now empty plate. "You didn't think I made that food, did you? And I work for the Somalis in their *spaza* in Alexandra and, well, I don't always have someone to look after Tsepo and Rasta. I can't take them with me, and I don't like to leave them here alone."

I see the opportunity and grab it. "We need a place to sleep. We'll get our own food, but we need a place to stay."

Catarina laughs. "We've got a bright boy here," she says. "You don't even have to ask him and he's bargaining already."

"So the strays are making demands now," says the woman called Angel. She walks up to the table and starts making herself tea. "We don't want to attract too much attention, Gawalia. The more people in the bridge, the more other people will notice. You know that?"

"We will be careful," I say, but she is not talking to me.

She smiles at me sweetly. "Careful of what, sugar cheeks?

You don't even know what's going on here. When did you arrive? A week ago, two weeks? You don't know how dangerous this place is becoming."

The couple and Gawalia exchange glances. The children on the bed let out happy squeals as they beat Innocent again. Angel spoons sugar into her mug and stirs it. This time she's the one who raises her eyebrow at Gawalia. I sense the opportunity slipping away. Nothing has been decided yet, but if I don't speak up now, it will be too late. I know how adults can sometimes speak to one another without talking.

"I'll be careful about coming in and out of the bridge," I say, looking squarely at Angel. "I will not bring trouble. Innocent is no problem to handle. I see what you have here, and you don't need to worry."

Angel holds my gaze for a moment and then shrugs, sipping her tea.

"It's your decision, Gawalia," she says. "You found this place. I'm just warning you. The more people we let in, the more trouble may come with them. I thought we all agreed that we were enough."

"What about your clients?" asks Catarina. "They come and go all the time."

"My clients are temporary. None of them stays here, you know that. Nobody sleeps with Angel."

"Well, the boys need someone to look after them, and Catarina and I can't be here all the time," says Rais.

"Rais, I'm not fighting with anyone, I'm just saying..." Angel doesn't finish her sentence.

We are all watching Innocent playing with the children. Tsepo is sitting in his lap and showing him how to shuffle the cards. Rasta hangs around Innocent's neck, laughing into his ear. Gawalia considers the scene on the bed for a moment longer, and then, making up his mind, he turns to me.

"Let's try it for a couple of weeks. You and Innocent look after Tsepo and Rasta during the day, and in exchange I'll give you a place to sleep. That's all we have here."

The four adults wait for my answer. Glancing over at my brother, there's not much to think about.

"I will help you, Gawalia. Innocent and I would love to look after your children while you are at work."

"Good," says Gawalia, and I realize then that he and the others are more relieved than I am. "From now on you can call this bridge your home."

18

LIFE IN A BRIDGE

Living inside a bridge is fine. And after living inside the bridge for five months you get used to the smell, the long shadows, and the intimate sounds of people. When we first arrived Gawalia helped us make our own section in the bridge. After a couple of weeks we found a mattress in the city dump that we brought back and stuffed through the hole. Catarina gave us our own paraffin lamp, which we hung from a nail in the cement ceiling, and Rais brought Innocent a bigger radio. Angel gave us some blankets. I found some cardboard boxes to use as insulation, and soon we were very cozy in our bridge called home, but I had no idea that looking after Tsepo and Rasta would be such hard work.

Gawalia explained in his gentle manner that everyone had to earn a living, and so if we all performed our duties, every-one's life would be more comfortable.

Catarina brought food back from the restaurant where she worked, so there was always something to eat.

Rais dealt with our security. He chased away anyone who stayed too long under the bridge. Gawalia hated rats, and so he made sure that we never left any food around. He was always sweeping out the dust through the hole, patching up damp spots and throwing out the dirty water.

Innocent played games with Tsepo and Rasta, bathed them at night, taught them how to read words in the newspapers, and basically kept them out of trouble. I don't think he saw it as work at all.

Once a day I was in charge of getting fresh water to the bridge. I filled a five-liter drum every morning from the community tap in Alexandra. Rais showed me where he hid a wheelbarrow to carry the empty drum to the township. I would wait my turn in the line and then wheel the full drum back to the bridge. Innocent would throw down a rope from the hole, and together we would pull it up into the bridge. The rest of the time I kept an eye on Innocent and the boys.

Angel always provided spare cash for emergencies. She did all her business with her cell phone. I would hear the familiar ringtone and know that in ten minutes one of her clients would appear under the bridge. In the late afternoon and early evening they would follow her past our sections to her side of the bridge. I never asked what she did with her clients, but I had a pretty good idea. Nobody spoke about it, which was fine with me. I just thought of the men as sad ghosts.

*   *   *

At Gawalia's table, I'm staring at the number I've written down on a piece of paper and at Angel's cell phone as she comes toward me. She is tying up her hair and rubbing the back of her neck. "I've got to do something about that bed. It's giving me neck ache," she says, scooping up some clean water from the drum. She expertly lights the paraffin burner and starts boiling water.

"So, you still haven't made that call?" she asks, spooning her usual three teaspoons of sugar into a cup and sitting down at the table.

"What if he's there? What do I say to him?"

"Hello, this is your son speaking," she answers flippantly. "Don't worry about that. Let the conversation take care of itself."

I told Angel about Innocent's wish to find our father. She said I could use her cell phone to call the work number that Innocent remembers.

"He probably doesn't work there anymore," I say, spinning the cell phone on the table.

"So, why not phone and find out? Oh, I get it. You're scared that if he doesn't work there anymore, you will have lost the possibility of finding him. Sometimes the wishing is better than the having. Believe me, I know what that is all about."

"It's a little of that, and a little of not wanting to lie to Innocent," I say, looking at my brother, who is reading a book with Tsepo and Rasta on our bed.

"Hey, you want me to try?" Angel picks up her phone and dials the number. She starts to hand the phone to me, but I shake my head. "What's his name again?"

"Mr. Goniwe."

"Hello, yes, I wonder if you can help me," she says. "I want to speak to Mr. Goniwe. Yes, I understand he is an employee of Removals. Mr. Goniwe." Angel rolls her eyes at me and makes a spinning gesture with her index finger. "She's checking," she whispers.

We wait. I can't stop my leg shaking. In a few moments I might be speaking to my father.

"Yes, I'm still here. Samuel Goniwe. Yes, that's right." Angel shrugs at me and I nod my head.

Samuel. That's my father's first name. I wonder if Innocent knew that.

"Oh," says Angel.

I watch her carefully. She turns away from me. "Okay. And you have no contact information? Yes, of course I know that, but could you check? I'm not asking a lot!" she says sharply. "Well, thank you very much!"

Angel snaps her cell phone shut and slips it into her pocket. "The bitch said that Mr. Goniwe hasn't worked there in five years and was laid off. She has no forwarding address and didn't know where I could find him. Sorry, sugar, but it was a long time ago."

"That's okay." I crumple the piece of paper and throw it on the ground. "That's a number I don't have to remember anymore."

"Don't worry. There are plenty of other ways of tracing people...."

A sharp whistle interrupts. It's Gawalia's signal for trouble.

"Rais! Angel! Come down here! Quickly!"

Angel and I poke our heads through the hole.

"There's trouble in Alexandra. I need some help at Ahmed's *spaza*. Where's Rais?"

"Catarina and Rais aren't here," says Angel.

"I'll help," I say without a second thought, and I swing down to the ground. Gawalia's wheelbarrow is filled with foodstuffs from his *spaza*. We load everything into a box, and Angel pulls it back up into the bridge.

Innocent's head appears in the hole.

"Deo, where you going?"

"I'm going to help Gawalia at the *spaza*. I won't be long."

"I need some more batteries, Deo."

"Okay, okay, I'll see you later."

I fetch my hidden wheelbarrow and follow Gawalia into Alexandra. He jogs ahead of me, pushing his empty wheelbarrow. There is no time to ask any questions.

A thick column of black smoke rises above the township. I catch a glimpse of orange flames. Perhaps someone is burning tires. A police van speeds past us in the direction of the flames. The wail of its siren makes me jump.

"Do you see the fire, Gawalia?" I shout.

"We're not going there. This way," he says, turning off the

road and heading down one of the side alleys into the heart of Alexandra.

People are out on the streets. They must have seen the smoke from the fire. They stand in groups talking, pointing in the direction of the speeding police van. I struggle to keep up with Gawalia. When we get to the shop, Ahmed, the owner, is outside looking up the street.

"Quickly, quickly," he shouts at Gawalia. "There is no time. They'll be here any minute."

Gawalia dashes into the shop and starts packing his wheelbarrow with foodstuffs. Meanwhile, Ahmed is shutting down the shop and pulling down the wire barricade in front of the windows.

I stand on the street catching my breath, watching people run past Ahmed's *spaza*. A man picks up a stone and throws it at Ahmed. It misses him, but the stone smashes through the glass window. The man shouts something I don't hear. Ahmed spins around, glass shattered all around him.

"What! Who did that?"

I point after the man running up the street. "What is going on?"

"Deo, help me," says Gawalia, shoving me roughly into the *spaza*, ignoring my question. "Take all the food on that shelf and pack it into your wheelbarrow. Fill your barrow only with as much as you think you can push."

I jump over the counter and pile up my wheelbarrow.

"You have to get out of here, Ahmed," says Gawalia.

"But it's my shop! What will I do? Why would they do this to me? We are neighbors!" Ahmed paces. He moves to the window, looks up and down the street.

"You must lock up and leave, now!" says Gawalia.

I run past the two of them carrying bags of rice and corn and cans of fruit and bottles of oil, trying to follow their conversation. It is strange to be raiding the *spaza*, carrying out all this stuff without paying for it.

"But it's not right!" shouts Ahmed.

"That doesn't matter now," says Gawalia. "We will take as much as we can and store it at the bridge. At least we can save some. Now you must go."

And that's when we hear ugly singing. And the loud voices of angry men shouting. And the screaming wail of police sirens.

Gawalia runs to the door and looks out at the street. "It's too late," he shouts. "Deo, come! Quickly!"

He slams the door of the *spaza* and locks it while Ahmed draws the curtains.

"What about our wheelbarrows?" I ask.

Again my question gets no answer. The walls of the shop shudder. A brick crashes through the window. Angry voices shout outside. Their words collide, fall over one another.

"All foreigners... out on the street, now!"

"Ahmed! We know you are in there. Come out, now."

"We are looking for foreigners!"

"Where is your country? Go home!"

"*Kwerekwere*, out now!"

The door shakes as it is beaten with a metal pole. The noise inside is deafening.

"I will speak to them," Ahmed says suddenly. "They will listen to me."

Gawalia grabs my arm and pushes me to the back of the *spaza*. He tries to stop Ahmed, but Ahmed is opening the door, shouting as he does so.

"Stop throwing rocks. I'm coming out!"

Hands grab Ahmed and pull him onto the street. He screams as many sticks fall on him. Another brick comes through the window. It lands at my feet. Ahmed's white robes turn red with blood. This is the last I see as Gawalia drags me away.

"Quick. We have to get out of here."

"What is going on, Gawalia?"

"They hate us. The people in Alexandra. They hate us foreigners. Come, run!"

We run into a backyard with a locked gate.

"Our wheelbarrows...the food..." I shout.

"Come on! There's no time." Gawalia climbs up on top of Ahmed's storeroom and reaches down for my hand. I scramble up and onto the roof and look out over the shacks of Alexandra.

"Look!" I shout, bewildered and scared by what I see.

More fires. Smoke pours from burning shacks. Gunshots

crack the air. Sirens sound everywhere. People run down the alleyways, chased by men carrying sticks and axes. Nobody has seen us on the roof, but soon someone will.

"We have to get out of here," says Gawalia, panic in his voice as we feel the chaos around us.

"This way," I say, leaping from the roof.

We race through the alleys, scramble over fences, dodge behind huts, keeping away from the main streets. All around us people are fleeing. Some carry crying children on their backs, some carry suitcases and parcels of clothing. Their fear is like flames. It jumps from person to person. The fear eats at us, burns us.

"Where are the *kwerekwere*?"

"We will kill all *kwerekwere*."

"Run! You are not wanted here."

More people come out of their shacks; it is better to be running than burning in your home. They run in every direction. Nobody knows where the men with sticks and axes will be. The ugly noise is everywhere.

We work our way back to the bridge, shack by shack, street by street, but we still have to cross the main entrance into Alexandra. I climb over a fence and cut across a backyard. Through a window of a shack I see the frightened faces of three children and a woman. She seems to be shouting something to me, but I can't hear her. I see only the flame of fear in her eyes. She is pointing toward the front door, but I have no time to listen to what she has to say. Gawalia pushes me onward. I run past the shack to the main road leading into Alexandra — and stop dead still.

Coming down the road is the mob of men, chanting the dreadful songs that send people running. Some wave axes and machetes above their heads. Some flick whips, which quiver like striking black puff adders. Some beat sticks against the lids of garbage cans.

Men and women run past me. Stones land around me. A woman is struck in the back and she screams, stumbles. I run to help her, but before I reach her, a gunshot explodes. The sound jerks her onto her feet, and she is running again.

People scatter in all directions. Women scream.

And the men with hatred in their faces are singing, singing, "Away with foreigners, kill the *kwerekwere*."

They keep going, heading toward our bridge. Toward our home.

19

NIGHT AT THE CHURCH

W e have to get back to the bridge," I say.

"Tsepo and Rasta," says Gawalia. "I've got to get them out."

Innocent.

These men will hurt my brother. He will not understand their questions. They will beat him. Kill him. I run down the road, dart back into the alleys. Fear drives me to run faster. I jump over fires that burn in the middle of the road, pushing past people, running as fast as I can to get ahead of the mob.

Gawalia follows. We are in sight of our bridge and see smoke rising beside the highway.

"No!" I scream, running to our entrance.

The highway is strangely empty. Where is the usual stream of cars? Have the police stopped the cars coming along this road? The smoke comes from a mattress that is burning next to the road. It is not the only thing from our home. The deck chairs, the blankets, the sheets, the food all lie scattered on the ground.

I spot the smashed remains of Innocent's radio.

We are too late.

"Innocent!" I scream, climbing up into the hole. "Innocent!"

Inside the bridge there is no light. Gawalia climbs up behind me and stumbles to the table. He lights the paraffin lamp. The place is a mess.

"Tsepo! Rasta!" he shouts.

There is no sign of Innocent or the two boys.

"Angel took them somewhere," says Gawalia.

"Maybe they are with Rais and Catarina."

We scramble down the hole, back to the ground.

"If they knew what was happening and they got away, where would they have gone?"

Gawalia doesn't answer me. He walks up to the road, looking carefully in both directions. "Come on," he says, "let's get out of here."

We run across the empty highway and scramble up the embankment, leaving Alexandra behind. We are not alone. There is a river of people crossing the highway and running away from Alexandra. Police vans speed past, lights flashing and sirens blaring.

"Maybe they've gone to the police station," says Gawalia.

The police station is swamped with people who have escaped from Alexandra. People spill out onto the pavement, blocking the traffic, crowding into the parking lot. A policeman is shouting at everyone to clear the entrance, but no one listens. We are all too shocked. Gawalia and I move through the crowds looking for Rais, Catarina, Angel — anyone who can tell us where Innocent and Tsepo and Rasta are.

Nobody knows whom we are talking about.

I have really lost Innocent this time. I have lost my brother. I have taken him from Gutu into a strange land, only to lose him. What would my mother think? How could I have been so careless? My hands sweat; a snake crawls in my stomach. Innocent lost.

"I've spoken to some people. They say there are a lot more people at the Methodist church grounds. Perhaps they are there," says Gawalia. His face is pressed with fear and worry about his sons.

"Let's go," I say. "Which way?"

"Follow me."

We run.

The Methodist church grounds are overflowing with even more people. They sit on the steps of the church, guarding their possessions, and some of them line up in front of a table where helpers are handing out tea and bread.

"Let's split up," says Gawalia. "I'll meet you back here in ten minutes."

I wander from group to group looking for Innocent, looking for anyone from the bridge. I ask people if they have seen two small boys and my brother. People ignore me or shake their heads. They have their own worries.

"How do we know we are safe here?" I overhear one of them say.

"Where are the police? Why are they not here to protect us?"

"They will come to this place. They will kill us all."

"We've done nothing to them. Why is this happening?"

Their words make no difference to me. I have lost Innocent. I'm sure more than ten minutes have passed, and I go to look for Gawalia.

I find him and start crying. "Where can he be, Gawalia?"

He has no answer. He pulls me close, holding me tightly.

We spend the night in the church grounds. It is not safe to leave, we are told. Gawalia talks to anyone who listens, asking about his sons. People shake their heads sadly. Someone offers him a cell phone to make a call to Angel. He calls, but her phone goes to voice mail. He tells her where we are and how she can find us.

Exhausted, we sleep on the ground.

I wake up in the night, and the thought that Innocent is lost crushes me. In the gloom of the church lights, I see bundles of people asleep on the ground. At the entrance to the church, a group of men stands watch. A police van is parked across the road, its blue and white lights revolving slowly, casting shadows on the wall.

I wander over to the tap against the church wall. I drink the cool water, splash some over my face.

Is this place worse than Gutu? Did I go through everything only to lose my brother in South Africa? I should have stayed in Gutu. I should have stayed in Bikita. I should have stayed in Beitbridge. I should have stayed at the Flying Tomato

Farm. None of this would have happened if I had not felt like we had to keep moving.

Try to think like Innocent, I say to myself. What would he do? Where would he go? He would stay with the people he knows. Rais, Catarina, or Angel. He would stick to them like glue. He must be with them.

I think about going back to the bridge. It's the middle of the night. Maybe he is waiting there. Surely it will be safe to go back now? But how will I find my way back in the night? It was daylight when we ran here; what if I got lost?

I return to where Gawalia is sleeping. Tomorrow we will find Rais or Catarina. Angel will answer her phone. Tomorrow everything will return to normal.

I lie down and pray for sleep to come.

In the morning, Gawalia and I go back to the police station. There are more people on the steps than the previous day. Shelters have been set up against the wall. A man is handing out parcels of food from the back of a truck. A team of people is putting up white tents in a field opposite the station.

We wander through the crowd of frightened people, checking faces, asking questions. I have never spent a night without my brother before. I keep turning around expecting to find Innocent standing close to me.

All morning, we wait in the line at the police station. When we finally get to the counter inside, we fill out a missing persons form. I look at the questions and know that this is not going to find Innocent. I leave the office and wait for Gawalia outside.

The morning's news from Alexandra is bad. Yesterday the police fought running battles with the *kwerekwere* killers, trying to restore the peace. I half listen to their stories, watching the street carefully, checking each new arrival for Innocent: the only face that will bring me peace.

At three o'clock Catarina and Rais come down the road, carrying Rasta and Tsepo. Gawalia cries out in relief as the boys run into their father's arms. Over the crush of talking and laughing I ask, "Where's Innocent?"

Catarina turns to me. "Deo, when we heard the gunshots we all got out of the bridge as fast as we could."

She looks at Rais.

"I grabbed the kids and Innocent," adds Rais. "We crossed the highway and went to the Community Center. People said it wasn't safe to go to the police station."

"But where's Innocent now?"

"He came with us," says Rais. "Really, Deo, he was with us."

"Rais, where is my brother?"

"He didn't want to stay at the Community Center. He went mad when we told him that he had to stay with us. He wanted you. He started screaming," says Rais.

"He wanted his Bix-box," says Catarina.

"You forgot to take his Bix-box? He never goes anywhere without that. You know that!"

"Deo, you're shouting. Calm down," says Gawalia.

I shrug Gawalia's hands off me.

Stupid. Stupid. Stupid. How could they not check if he had his Bix-box? Of course he would go mad.

"Where did he go?" I demand, but neither Rais nor Catarina answers. Tsepo starts crying.

"Innocent went back," the little boy says. "To fetch his box. He told me."

"You let him go back to the bridge? Alone?"

"The boys, Deo, we had to look after them.... W-we couldn't stop him," says Catarina, stuttering. "We were frightened."

We both know what might have happened to Innocent. I see it in her eyes.

"He wouldn't listen. He ran away," says Rais, raising his hands as if he had just given up.

"You never give up with Innocent. Of course he didn't listen to you, Rais. You gave up on him," I say.

These people do not understand my brother the way I do. How can they? I turn to leave.

"No, Deo, you can't. It's too dangerous. Wait until the police have..."

But I know what I have to do, and no one will stop me.

20

BURNT GARBAGE

I must go carefully, with eyes in the back of my head. The men in Alexandra will kill me if they catch me, but I must go back to the bridge. That is the place Innocent knows, and that is where he will be. He will be waiting for me at the bridge we call home.

I dash across the street, dodging the cars, and run along the pavement. The afternoon sky is dark with the smoke of fires that still blaze. Ash catches in my throat. The smell of burning tires makes me thirsty.

The more ground I cover, the more confident I become. I know I will find Innocent. He would never go somewhere strange without me. I've told him that if he gets lost he must return to the place we were last together. I know he will be waiting for me at the bridge.

Wait for me, wait for me, is the beat in every step that I make, the prayer of every breath that I take. I run along the road toward the bridge. I slip past a roadblock set up to stop cars from going into the township.

Once on the top of the bridge, I scramble down the side and kick through the remains of our home. I find my soccer pouch and stuff it into my pocket.

"Innocent!" I shout up into the hole.

I clamber up and stand in the semidarkness inside the bridge.

"Innocent!" There is no answer.

Nothing stirs.

And then a match is struck, its tiny light massive in the darkness. I stumble toward the light. "Innocent, I knew I would find you. I was so worried...."

The light comes from the other end of the bridge. The sheet glows yellow in front of the flickering flame. I hear a groan as I move the sheet aside.

"Deo?"

It is Angel.

Angel is covered with blood, beaten. She lies on her bed, curled up in a ball. Her face is swollen. Her eyes are slits in puffed-up balls.

"Angel, what happened?" I kneel next to her, afraid to touch her.

She raises her hand slowly, moving my question away. "They were tired of paying a *kwerekwere*. They wanted it for free," she says, with a laugh that sounds more like a choke.

"Where's Innocent?"

"He tried to stop them. He tried to help me. They took him outside."

I back away from her. I swing through the hole back to the ground. He tried to stop them. They took him outside.

I climb the embankment back up to the road and look toward Alexandra. Two police vans have parked next to each other a short distance away on the Alexandra side of the bridge. They have to help me. I run toward them.

Two policemen stand smoking, leaning against the front of the vehicles, their backs to me. A loud voice shocks me back to reality. It comes from the two-way radio in the police van. The men ignore the crackle and conversation from their radio.

Then I see Innocent's Bix-box lying on the ground next to a pile of burnt garbage.

They must have found Innocent! He must be in the back of one of their vans. I quickly look inside the one van. Not here. The other van.

Not here either.

I walk around the van to pick up Innocent's Bix-box.

"Hey, boy, get out of here. This is no place for you," says one of the men, flicking his cigarette to the ground.

"I have to get that box. It belongs to my brother," I say, pointing at the tin box and staring at the garbage that isn't garbage at all.

"Get out of here!"

And as he grabs me, I see the shape of a human head, lying on its side. The shape of an arm and a hand, stretched out toward the Bix-box.

I don't feel myself falling, but I fall.

I don't feel myself crying, but I cry.

I don't hear myself screaming, but I scream.

I don't feel the hands trying to stop me from going to Innocent, but somehow I reach the body of my brother, facedown on the ground, covered with rubble.

Then I stop screaming, stop crying, stop seeing...and feel nothing.

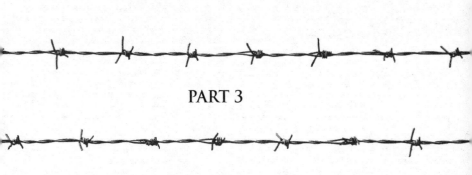

PART 3

UNDER
A TABLE
MOUNTAIN

(EIGHTEEN MONTHS LATER)

21

COMING DOWN

The ball sails toward me, carried by the wind. It moves slowly in the air, spinning and rotating. I wish it would leave me alone.

I used to know what to do with a soccer ball heading my way. I watch how it spins through the air: a new, shiny, black-and-white soccer ball. In another four seconds it will strike some part of my body. Maybe it will hit my face. Maybe it will hit my arm, my chest, or my leg.

I don't care.

I sit under a highway that snakes its way into the city. The cars speeding above me are so far away, like the cliffs of Table Mountain rising a mile high into the sky. All I am capable of at the moment is sitting, my head against a wall, coming down from a glue-tube high, where the world is unbearably light, slow, and very bright. The glue makes everything weightless; I am no longer heavy with memory and guilt. In my glue-tube world there are no decisions to take, no plans to make.

But coming down is the worst time. The world comes into focus again. My muscles start aching. I begin to feel my tongue. I might have to stick my finger down my throat and vomit. I usually feel better after that. My thoughts turn into heavy, fat balloons of words.

Memories return. Guilt cramps.

I am thirsty and hungry, all at the same time. Nothing new about that. My stomach aches. I've started feeling again. Like shit. Always like shit.

Sooner or later I'm going to have to find another magic tube. The others will help me. They know where to get the stuff that keeps everything nicely out of focus, nicely slow and light. They left me when I passed out under the highway — maybe it was last night?

I am alone now. Nothing new about that either anymore. I have learned to be alone. You use people when you need them, and you leave them when you don't. I meet people and I leave them. That is how it has always been with me.

I left Amai and Grandpa Longdrop, Captain Washington, Gawalia, Tsepo and Rasta. I left Rais and Catarina. I left Angel.

When the government closed down the camp at the Methodist church in Jozi, the people of the bridge had to make one of two decisions: go back home or go back to the bridge. We had spent four months in the camp — a place of plastic food, leaky tents, and officials with notebooks — and we knew it was time to go. Many people wanted to stay in the tents, but the officials said it was safe to go home.

I had no home to go back to. And I would not go back to the bridge. So I took a train and crossed a desert and ended up beside the sea at a Camp called Sea Haven. Running can take you a long way, but I can run no farther because of the sea. The blue line of the watery horizon can't be reached by running straight ahead. In my worst moments, I've thought about running into the sea and searching for the life after this one. But I'm not ready to end my life. Not yet.

Not like Muhammad, the Somali man who had had enough of the camp.

"They dropped us off at the end of the world," Muhammad said to me, his shawl wrapped around his shoulders against the cold as we stared out at the angry waters only a few feet away from the tents. "What do you see behind us, Deo?"

"Tents and police vans," I answered.

"Suffering, Deo. People suffering. That is what is behind us."

He was right. I had seen enough suffering at the camp in Johannesburg and this one in Cape Town to know what he was talking about.

"And in front of you?" he asked again.

"The sea," I said.

"No, Deo. There is nothing in front of us. Our lives end here at the end of the world. To lose your dreams is one thing, but to lose your place in the world…" Muhammad shook his head and sighed. "We do not belong anywhere, Deo. We have no future."

Muhammad had had enough of what he called a life without hope and without country. He couldn't leave Sea Haven, so he chose to run to the blue horizon. They sent out a boat to fetch him, but they never found him.

The ball has not reached me yet. Why does it take so long to travel through the air? I should move, but that will take effort.

"When you wake up in the morning, are you Deo first, or are you a refugee?" asked the pretty young woman from the United Nations, staring at me from behind her smart glasses and writing down everything I said.

"I am a refugee," I answered her. "How can I be anything else? Everywhere I look reminds me that this is not my home. The truth is in the pots they dish our food from, in the mat I sleep on, the blankets, in the tents. It is in the food I eat, in the water I drink, and in the look in your eyes — it's in everything. I don't want to be called a refugee, but how can I change what I am?"

After Muhammad sank beneath the waters, searching for the blue horizon, I knew I could not stay in Sea Haven. I heard the promises of the government, listened to the words of the officials of the United Nations, but I could hear no truth in them. They did not know what to do with us. Then the storm blew down the tents, and the blue-uniformed police came and told everyone to leave. We had to reintegrate, we were told.

How?

Nobody could answer that question. We had to return to our countries, they said.

How?

They had no answers to that one either. So I ran again. The streets in the city are warmer than the tents of Sea Haven. Here you are free and nobody tells you what to do, what to eat, where to sleep. Here you can get whatever you want. Here everything is possible.

The ball is closer now.

I think it will hit my cheek in about two seconds. I'll wait and see what will happen. That's how it has been so far. Things happen to me; I'm forced to react.

I have to get up, move, join the others. I will not be alone for long. The others will come back when they are hungry and need someone to do the running.

That's what I'm good at — running.

When I run from a shop, no one can catch me. It's the easiest thing in the world to walk into a shop and fill up a basket and then run. I dodge past people, feint this way, that way, and then sprint across the street, leaving anyone foolish enough to run after me puffing and panting behind.

*　　*　　*

Finally the ball smashes into my cheek. It stings like a slap in the face. I shake my head, lift my hand to my cheek.

But there are more balls. The air is filled with two more. No, now there are three, four, even more, flying through the air. They bounce around me like giant hailstones. I blink several times. The glue-tube must still be working its magic.

I can't believe what I am seeing, yet my cheek stings, so I must have been struck by one of these balls. I stand up. Where have these balls come from? Why are they flying toward me?

I aim at the wall holding up the highway, striking angrily at the ball that hit me in the face. My kick is solid. The ball springs from my foot, flies toward the wall. It bounces back to me. I strike it again, this time with my left foot. It flies away again, heading back toward the wall, but then, as if reminding me of something I have long forgotten, it returns to me. The ball will not let me go. It demands that I do something.

I remember.

I head the ball. Once, twice, three times in the air, watching it carefully as it bounces off my forehead. Now the ball is in my control. It listens to me. It will not strike me in the face again. I let it drop onto my knee and then bounce it to my other knee. I swivel, shifting my weight onto my left leg, and catch the ball with my right, kicking it in the sweet spot, sending it back to the wall.

The satisfying sound of ball against wall, hitting the exact spot I aimed at. Yes, that feels good. I do it again and again, striking the ball harder and harder against the wall. And each time it returns to me, as I know it will.

This I can depend on.

I remember how to run with the ball at my feet, how to pass it from one foot to the other, how to lift it up in mid-run and flick it past my opponent. I dribble the ball around the other balls that have now come to a rest under the highway. I line up the shot, lead with my left foot, and deliver a powerful kick that sends the ball curling through the air straight back at the wall.

I lift my hand in the air, acknowledging the applause. But there can be no applause. I am alone.

I spin around.

A man is applauding me. At his feet is a net-bag full of soccer balls. There is a laughing tiger tattoo on his neck. A silver whistle glints on his chest. He has a funny expression on his face.

"And you? Beckham under a bridge. Where did you learn to play soccer?"

His words come from a long way off. I stare at him, feeling the world slow down to a blur. I say nothing. The tiger on his neck laughs at me. He looks like one of the others but for his smart tracksuit, the whistle, and white sneakers. I cannot explain to him where I learned to play soccer. He would never understand.

"What's your name?"

"I am a refugee."

He laughs. "But you have a name?"

I shrug. It's time to run. I should come down alone. Find the others. I turn away.

"Wait! Where do you think you're going? Do you want to play soccer?"

I stop. The stranger lifts his net-bag full of soccer balls as if he is offering them to me. The tiger on his neck winks at me; the whistle blinks.

"So you think you're hot? Show me what you've got." He takes out one of the balls and rolls it to me. I do what the ball asks me to do, kicking it straight back at this man, aiming for his net of balls. The balls explode out of his net with the force of my shot.

"Phew! So you've got a mean right foot. Good. That's good. Come with me, if you want to play," he says.

I have to do something, so I go with him.

22

STREET SOCCER

We have enough, Salie! We agreed on twenty. That's all we can afford, remember?"

"I know what we said, but just one more, Tom. That's all I'm asking for — just one more."

"That's what you said when we agreed on a pretrial squad of four teams, and then suddenly it became five teams, and now you want one more player...."

"Tom, he's something special, I can feel it. You know how I found him?"

"Oh no, you're not going to tell me another miracle story...."

"I was late, going too fast on the highway, and somehow the balls got loose in the back of the truck. As I came down the off-ramp, they went flying, most of them landing under the highway. I drove around to collect them, and there was this boy, hammering balls against the wall, dribbling and bouncing balls from knee to knee like David Beckham."

I guess he's talking about me.

And here I am in the Hartleyvale Stadium changing room. I can't stop my hands shaking long enough to tie up my shoelaces. Salie gave me boots, socks, a T-shirt, and shorts. He told me to get dressed quickly; we were late for practice. Now if only I could tie these laces!

Coming down is bad. You get the shakes, your stomach cramps up, and you're hungry enough to eat anything. I've got to get some of the magic tube soon, or I'll be a real mess.

"You're sure he's sixteen years old?"

"Yes. He's old enough." Salie bangs on the door of the changing room. "Come on, Deo! Let's move."

I give up trying to tie the laces and stuff them into my socks. I join the men waiting for me outside the changing room.

"Deo, this is Tom Galloway. He's the manager, team doctor, resident physical therapist, and part-time psychologist." Salie laughs.

A gray-haired, red-faced barrel of a man puts out his hand. "Hello, Deo. Welcome. I'm looking forward to seeing you play," he says, shaking my hand as if to break every bone in the process. "You look a bit unwell. Are you all right?"

"I'm fine," I say quickly. I play it straight—sad face, hopeful eyes, crooked little smile. I know how to get a free meal: look pathetic and keep it together.

Tom shoots Salie a glance, shakes his head, and stomps away. The old fart didn't buy what I was selling. I'll have to watch him.

"Don't worry about him," says Salie. "He's tough to begin with, but you start scoring goals and he'll like you soon enough."

I just nod and follow Salie into the stadium. I get a closer look at the laughing tiger on his neck. There are more symbols on his arms, blue lines carved into his skin.

"Where did you get that?" I ask, pointing at the tiger.

"In another life. You've seen it before?"

"On the streets — those that have been to prison..."

"I've been where they've been, but now I'm here. Look."

The soccer field is enormous, green and empty, the goal post un-netted.

"We don't practice there," he says. "We're playing street soccer, so we practice on a cement court."

The soccer arena behind the stadium is both familiar and strange. The cement playing area is the size I'm used to. It's about twenty steps long and fifteen steps wide. But instead of an imaginary goal, on either side of the court there is a real netted goal. It's about four steps wide but no higher than the normal height of a person. The strangest part is the four-feet-high boards surrounding the cement court. What's that about?

"You've never seen a street soccer game before?"

"'Course I have," I lie.

Salie blows sharply on his whistle, and those running around the court turn and head over to us. Everyone is wearing the same clothes.

"This is Deo, everyone, and he's the reason I'm late," Salie says.

I flick over the twenty blank faces, their eyes drilling through me. They're not impressed with me, but why should I care? I notice the pale yellow moon-shaped shadows around some of their eyes—we've got some glue-tube heads here. Their eyes glint with the hard life on the streets. The cold pavement's been their pillow often enough. Some of them have tattoos of street gangs, and I know what shit they've had to do to be part of a gang.

"That's not fair, Salie, he didn't come through the trials," says one boy. He is taller and older than the rest. He has a scar down the side of his neck, and his eyes are ringed with shadows.

"No, he didn't, T-Jay, because he's a coach's choice. Do you have a problem with that?"

"We all had to come through the trials. You just picked him up—"

"Off the streets, T-Jay," interrupts Salie. "Just like every one of you."

The boy called T-Jay hesitates, shoots me an evil look, and shuts up.

"Are we going to stand around and talk all day, or are we going to play? I'm sick and tired of doing laps," says a dark-haired girl standing at the back with her hands on her hips.

"We're going to play, Keelan," says Salie. "Teams A and D get the first fourteen minutes. C and B teams, warm up."

The group breaks up and heads toward the benches. I follow Salie. He points to a raised bench outside the court.

"Sit, watch, and learn, Deo. I'll play you in the second game," he says, entering the court with a ball under his arm.

The goalies each take up their positions. It's a four-person-a-side game: striker, two wings, and a goalie. Salie blows his whistle and rolls the ball into the middle of the court, and the game is on.

The play is fast and furious. Instantly I see what the boards surrounding the court are used for: deflection. Players slam the ball against the boards, timing their pass to connect with someone moving up the court. The boards add a new dimension to the game—like a reliable fifth player who never makes a mistake. The players stay out of a half-moon penalty box and shoot only from a fair distance.

Despite the tremor in my hands and the dull ache in my stomach, I can't wait to play. I manage to tie my shoelaces just as Salie blows his whistle and the players come off the court.

"Deo, you're up," calls Salie. "It's a fourteen-minute game. Let's see what you've got."

Everybody watches me walk onto the court. I don't care what they think. The goalie on the other team slaps his hand and crouches in his goal. It will be tough to get the ball past him.

"I'm Keelan," says the dark-haired girl. "And yes, I'm on your team, so you can close your mouth."

"I'm Jacko," says a boy, grinning at me. "Try not to get in the way, Deo."

"Okay, let's play, you guys. Somebody mark T-Jay! I don't want any slackers on this team. Keelan! Stop making eyes at the new boy and get into position. Jacko, come back! You're too far forward," shouts the goalkeeper.

"That's Alfabeto. He's a motormouth," says Keelan. "He won't stop talking and yelling the whole game. You'll get used to it."

Salie blows his whistle — game on. As quickly as the ball is passed to me, it is taken off me by T-Jay. He flicks the ball against the side board and is about to shoot when Keelan intercepts, and the ball is back at my feet.

My head is spinning; sweat runs down my face. I run, pass, tackle, run, and gasp for air. Sometimes the ball is connected to me by elastic; at other times it feels like a block of wood. I haven't played for a long time, and never like this. I breathe heavily, sweat streaming down my face. At last the one-minute break is called, and I bend over, feeling the familiar pain in my side.

"You okay, Deo?" asks Keelan, smiling.

I feel terrible. "I'm fine," I snap.

The second half is better. Something of the way I used to play returns. I catch T-Jay with the ball and win it from him cleanly, bounce it off the wall past the defender, and aim left with a clear shot at the goal. I prepare to shoot with my right foot, and then in a split second I move the ball to my left and power in a low curling shot that flies past the goalie.

From somewhere far away I hear, "*Gooooaal*," and then the world spins around me and I hit the cement.

"Deo, are you okay?"

"He's got the shakes. He's a glue-boy."

"Somebody bring the stretcher!"

"Deo? Deo, can you hear me?"

I want to answer, but darkness won't let me.

I wake up thirsty.

I sit up, and someone puts a water bottle into my hands. I drink and drink and drink. Water spills down my front. We are in the change-room.

"Take it easy, Deo. Slowly, slowly."

Salie's face comes into focus; his tiger is still laughing. This is it. I will be thrown out. He knows what I am. I am nothing to him, nothing to anyone. So what? I can give back the boots, shorts, socks, T-shirt, and return to the streets.

"Hey, Deo, listen to me," says Salie firmly. He gets up to close the door, and then sits on a bench next to me. "You see this?" He points at his neck. "He's laughing at you 'cause you fell off his back. Life is a tiger, and you've got to ride him and hold on and never let go. I know what I'm talking about. I kicked a ball under the streetlights of Hanover Park and wanted to be the next Pelé. But the gangs found me and took me on a different path. Hey, are you listening?" He cuffs me gently on the back of my head. Nobody touches me, but I don't mind Salie. There is gentleness in his eyes.

"Yes," I say, rubbing the back of my head.

"Good, 'cause this is how it's going to work. I am preparing three teams for the Street Soccer World Cup tournament in Cape Town a month before the World Cup kicks off in South Africa. It's my job to prepare a team of twelve players who will play against forty-eight teams from all around the world.

"The other players are just like you—they're homeless, or in drug or alcohol rehab, or asylum seekers.

"You want to be in my training camp, you've got to do two things: get off glue and stay off the streets. I'll help you get off glue, and Tom will put you up at the YMCA with the rest of the players. But only *you* can stay off the streets. I'll train you the best I can, but I don't take any *kak*. You understand? Salie's tiger will be watching you. It's your job to get fit enough to play.

"After a month you'll know if you're playing in the tournament. But if you want a chance to play, you're going to have to do as I say. So what's it going to be?"

"Okay." All it takes is one word. I'm not stupid. I know this is the best thing that has ever happened to me. "Okay," I say again, just to make sure Salie heard me. "Okay."

"Good, but I heard you the first time," he says, smiling.

23

PAINFUL PRACTICE

After ten nights of sharing a room and sleeping in a soft bed at the YMCA, I'm woken up by a knocking sound. I lie still, listening. There it is again, a quiet, determined *tap-tapping* at the window. I sit up in bed, glancing over at the other boys.

"Jacko," I whisper. "Are you awake? Alfabeto!"

I swing my legs off the bed and listen again. A stick is knocking on the pane of glass. I open the window and look out into the city night. Below, huddled closely together, is a group of hooded figures. The others have found me.

"Deo! I can see you. Get down here!" It's the raspy voice of one of the boys I knew on the streets. "We need you to run for us again."

I look at the upturned faces of the others, lit by the yellow glow from the streetlight. Even though the evening is mild, they are layered with clothing. One of them carries a cardboard box under his arm. I don't recognize all of them. That's how it is. They come and go.

"What time is it?" I whisper back as loudly as I dare. It's a dumb thing to ask, but I don't know what else to say.

"Get your ass down here," comes the answer. "We've got a job to do. I've also got this." He lifts up a familiar small pot. I hear someone stir behind me. Jacko rolls over in his sleep, mumbling.

Decision time. Nobody would know if I slipped back to the streets for a night, ran with the others until the early morning. I could be back in time for breakfast. My nose tingles at the memory of the glue and its numbing power. I need a break from the training. I don't belong anywhere; why should I think that I belong here?

And after what happened today on the soccer court, I have no reason to believe that anything will get better.

"Why don't we have a South Africa versus Foreigners game?" asked T-Jay earlier this afternoon, while we were taking a break on the stands.

His question came out of nowhere. Salie never asked any of us where we came from. He only wanted to see how we played. He knows at least seven of us are not South African, and of course he knows that all of us are wondering if only the locals will make the cut.

T-Jay's question sparked a flashing light somewhere in the back of my brain. There was an edge to his casual question, and I caught the knowing looks exchanged among the South Africans.

I glanced around to see what the others thought of his suggestion. There were a few embarrassed smiles, one or two nods, and an ever-so-slight cowering among the seven of us foreigners.

"That's not what Salie said," said Keelan. "We're supposed to work for an hour on the ball-control drill and then finish the practice with laps and the usual stretching exercises. We'd better do what he says, even if he isn't here watching."

"Ah, come on, Keelan, unless you're scared of being beaten and me running circles around your cute butt," said T-Jay. His challenge was light as a feather and as sharp as a razor.

"You know where you can put this?" said Keelan, showing T-Jay her middle finger.

"It will be fun," said Jacko. "We just might find some new combinations that Salie hasn't thought of yet. What do you say, Deo?"

I shrugged. "What do I care? You're crazy if you think the street-soccer South Africans are any better than the national side. Bafana Bafana won't make it through the first round in the World Cup. So what makes you think the street-soccer side will do any better?"

Well, that comment got up everyone's noses. There were howls of outrage and insults galore. In an instant, we were Foreigners and South Africans, Us and Them—the divide as sharp and high as the barbed-wire fence at the border.

I had Keelan from Kenya and Ernesto from Mozambique. Godfast, with hands the size of frying pans, was in goal. Godfast comes from northern Zimbabwe and is the best goalie in the training camp.

The game started out well enough, but after three minutes T-Jay's side went a goal down and things got rougher. No penalties were called, and there was more than the usual yelling and foul play.

Keelan is light and fast on her feet, and she ran rings around Jacko and T-Jay. So after they had been robbed of the ball once too often, Jacko charged her from behind and sent her sprawling onto the cement.

Then the game got ugly quickly. As much as the South African players tried, they couldn't get the ball past Godfast. He would pluck their shots out of the air with a broad grin and ask, "Is that the best you got, Banana Banana?"

After I scored our third goal, late in the second half, T-Jay lashed out at me with his elbow. The blow caught me squarely between the eyes, and for a moment I thought I was going to fall down. But instead of taking me down, it was like a switch that flicked on inside me. My fist found its way up T-Jay's nose and my knee said hello to his balls. I didn't care that he was bigger and older or that he got in quite a few good punches before my nose started bleeding. I stopped kicking T-Jay only when I heard Salie's whistle bursting my eardrum.

He was furious about the cause of the fight.

"What were you trying to prove, T-Jay?" he yelled. "That you're better than people who come from Mozambique, Zimbabwe, or DRC? What are the two things I've been drilling into every one of you? Discipline and respect. I'll have no street fighting in my camp. And, Deo, if you can't control your temper, you can leave right now!"

"Is this a South African street-soccer side or not?" yelled T-Jay back into Salie's face. "We have a right to know!"

"He's right, Coach," said Keelan. "If you're going to choose only players with a green ID, then what are the rest of us here for? Trainee punching bags for the South Africans?"

Finally, Us and Them were out in the open. Salie was a fool if he thought he could ignore what had happened. Us and Them were here to stay.

Salie spoke a whole lot of words, but none of them made any sense. He went on about being chosen on merit, saying we had all been found on the streets, and that was enough.

"Where you come from doesn't matter. Not for one moment," he added lamely.

"Oh yes it does," I shouted, wiping the blood from my nose. "I'm not a South African, and I don't plan on becoming one. In this country I am the lowest of the low because I come from Zimbabwe. Where you come from does matter — it matters a lot. You tell us we'll be playing against people from Brazil, Australia, Canada, and Denmark. You think these people don't care where they come from?"

Salie tried to answer me, but his words fell on deaf ears.

Something had been broken. At dinner, we foreigners sat at one end of the table, the South Africans at the other. Nothing had changed in my life; I was still an outsider.

"Deo, come on. We're waiting," calls the raspy voice from the street below. "We need you."

The night air is cool on my face. My nose tingles in anticipation of what the small pot offers. The hooded figures below become impatient; two of them slip away in the night. The leader raises the pot with his left hand and silently calls me to join them with his right. I catch his smile, turned yellow by the streetlight. It would be so easy to pack my stuff, slip away, glide down the hallway and out the door, and run again with them.

24

THE LAST DRILL

Salie works us hard for six straight days. We run endless drills, sweat out hundred-meter dashes, put in hours of weight work, and suffer through mind-numbing stretch exercises. When Alfabeto is brave enough to ask when we are actually going to play some soccer, Salie's reply is short and curt. "When I say so. Now get your head down and do two more laps."

He watches each of us closely, making notes in his book. On the fourth day he pulls three of the boys and one girl aside. They stand at the end of the court, deep in conversation. I notice that one by one, their heads drop, and Salie puts his hand on each of their shoulders. They leave and don't come back. Part of the deal of the training camp was that those who did not make it would be offered accommodation at a halfway house. At least they wouldn't have to go back to the streets. But that's little consolation. They didn't make it. That's got to hurt.

I keep my head down, work harder, stay out of trouble, and try not to catch Salie's eye. The next day, two more players are pulled out of the practice, and we look away, trying not to stare, as they are told they have to leave. Nobody talks about those who are gone. It's as if they were never here.

Then Salie makes each of us foreigners partner with a South African. T-Jay is my new stretch mate. We do weights together, we partner for all the soccer drills, and he gets to run across the field and up the stadium stands, carrying me on his back. Salie is sweating out all the trouble of a few days ago.

"We might as well be married," T-Jay grumbles over his shoulder as he struggles across the field under my weight.

"I don't like this either," I say, gripping him around his neck as I feel myself slipping down his back. "Shut up and hold me tighter."

"You see what I mean? We sound like we've been married for thirty years!"

That cracks us both up, and we fall down laughing in a heap in the middle of the field.

On the seventh day after the Us-Them blowup, Salie is waiting for us beside the court. "Follow me," he says, without any greeting.

We follow him into one of the conference rooms inside Hartleyvale Stadium, where the chairs have been arranged in a circle.

"Sit," says Salie, taking a piece of paper from his folder.

We don't dare look at one another. I can't look at Salie. He means business. Instead, I look at the tiger on his neck.

"On this piece of paper are the names of the players on this year's South African Street Soccer World Cup team."

This is the moment I've been dreading and hoping for.

"But before I read out the names, there's one last thing you have to do to get onto this team," Salie says, folding the paper and putting it in his top pocket. "You guys made me think a lot about what happened last week. I don't like to fail, but last week I failed you. I couldn't give you the answers you were looking for. I suppose because it's a tough subject, and it's something we don't like to talk about.

"I'm talking about xenophobia. You know what that word means? Being frightened of people who come from another country, and hating them because of it.

"You were right, T-Jay. This is the South African street-soccer side. We are entering the tournament representing South Africa. And you were right too, Deo. It does matter where you come from. It matters a lot.

"The problem is that I don't think we all understand what it means to be a South African, or what it means to live in this part of the world. Do any of you know how the person sitting next to you came to be here, in Cape Town?"

Nobody answers him. I've never heard Salie this serious before.

"For a long time, many people in this country thought

apartheid and segregation were the only way. And there were a lot of people who turned a blind eye to people who were suffering. Talk to me, talk to my father and his grandfather. We know about what happened in this country. And now, almost sixteen years after Mandela was president, we are making the same damn mistake again! We're ignoring the suffering of people who come from other African countries far worse off than our own."

He leans back in his chair and slowly scans every face in the room.

"Well, I'm not going to allow fear and hatred to mess up my team," he adds, smacking both of his knees and leaning forward.

"Today I want to hear your stories. You're going to tell me where you come from and how you got to be in this room today. And I want all of you to listen. Listen hard, and try to understand."

People shift uncomfortably in their seats. A few of the boys drop their heads to their chests. My palms go sweaty. The room is silent with tension.

"Think of this as your last drill," Salie says, patting his shirt pocket. "Who's going to go first?"

I glance around the circle. No one is really looking at anyone else. No one looks at Salie either. The ceiling and the floor have become the most fascinating things in the room, and the silence is like a big, fat balloon waiting to pop. Nobody wants to go first. Out of the corner of my eye, I catch

Salie folding his arms and leaning back in his chair, simply waiting.

"I will," says Keelan suddenly. She bites her bottom lip and thinks for a moment.

"My father was a social worker, working in Kamukunji, in Kenya. This was where I was born. The town is about two hundred miles from Nairobi." Keelan stops, drops her head, and grips the sides of her chair.

"Go on," says Salie.

"My father was a community leader. People trusted him. He was in charge of counting the votes for the election. I didn't know much about the election. I didn't care in the beginning. At first, everything was peaceful."

Keelan looks like she is holding on to Salie with her eyes. Her voice shakes. "My father was a Kikuyu. He believed we should vote for the party that would bring development to the region. He had counted the votes twice, and he knew who had won.

"Then the people who supported the government came to Kamukunji. They told my father and the community leaders that the outcome of the election must be that the president would win.

"These outside people did not like what my father said about how the people should vote. That night they started burning houses in Kamukunji. In the morning they came after my father. Luckily, my baby sister and I were with my mother at her family's house, so we didn't know what happened. But then my uncle came to tell us that our house had been burned down and that my father was dead.

"They had chopped off his arms with a machete. The people took him to the community hospital, but it was closed. My father died outside the hospital the next day. I wanted to see his body, but my mother said we had to leave, that it was not safe for us to live in Kamukunji anymore. My sister was too little to travel with us, so we left her with my aunt. My mother and I traveled through Nairobi into Tanzania. We got rides in delivery trucks to Botswana. We came to South Africa and stayed in Upington, but there was no work there. Then we came to Cape Town, where my mother worked at the harbor." Keelan's voice becomes very quiet. "Until she got sick and died."

No one seems to be breathing. Not even Salie.

"My father taught me to play soccer. We would watch Manchester United together on television. In Kamukunji, we went to the Methodist church each Sunday. So I went to the Methodists here after my mother died. They told me about the soccer trials, and that's how I came here."

Keelan's voice goes very small until it breaks. We all think that she is finished, but then she looks around at us all. "South Africa is very hard for me. Everything is different from the way it was in Kenya. I don't like asking for help, but I need money to go back to Kenya and fetch my sister. I want to bring her here to stay with me."

She drops her eyes away from Salie and swings her legs under her chair. She is finished. We all look at Salie.

"Thank you, Keelan. Who is next?"

This time it is not long before someone puts up his hand. Now it's T-Jay.

"I come from Steinkopf. I know, I know—nobody knows where that is. I call it the hairy armpit of South Africa—it's a town this side of the Namibian border close to the desert. No, it *is* the damn desert!

"My father worked for the old South African Defence Force as a tracker. He lost his job when he stood on a land mine. It blew off his foot."

Everyone laughs and T-Jay grins, shaking his head. "Don't laugh! It sounds like a joke, but it wasn't funny. He couldn't work anymore, so he stayed at home. He beat the crap out of me until the social services took him away. My mother says he was an alcoholic. We saw less and less of him until my mother said that he wouldn't be coming back.

"She said he had gone to Cape Town. So I ran away. That was pretty stupid. I was only thirteen. I think I wanted to find him. Even though he beat me, I felt sorry for him. He was a damn fine tracker until he lost his foot.

"I never found him in Cape Town, and when I realized that my old man was probably dead, it was too late to go back. My mother still lives in Steinkopf, but I don't hear from her much these days. I think it would be nice to have a brother or a sister—some sort of family, you know? You're lucky, Keelan, even if your sister isn't here.

"I could go back to Steinkopf, but there's nothing there for me. I suppose I should have gone to school, but it's too late for that now. I got into drugs," says T-Jay, looking quickly at Salie, who is nodding. "That was rough, but I'm through with that now. I never want to go back to that shit."

"Thank you, T-Jay," says Salie. "Who's next?"

And so it goes on, story after story, told by every person sitting in the circle. Some have their funny moments, all have their problems, and most of them are sad.

All of the people in the room have come from somewhere other than Cape Town. We are all strangers to this city, but none is a stranger to sadness and death.

All of the people in the room want to be somewhere else. None of us wants to live on the streets of Cape Town.

All of the people in the room want to belong somewhere and be treated as somebody, not something.

As each person speaks, the stories get easier to tell and easier to listen to. I notice too that as each of the people in the room talks, something changes in their faces. A light goes on in their eyes. It's like they were gray, but now they have color. No one is nervous anymore, and with the telling of each story, those who have not spoken get more confidence.

Each story is like the black-and-white patch of a soccer ball. Each one makes the ball whole.

"Deo? You are the last," says Salie. "It's your turn now."

I want to add my patch, but I cannot. I need to keep it to myself. I don't want to share it with anyone. My story is still in my head, buried. I cannot go back to what happened. I have already heard parts of my story in those who spoke before me. My story is all I have.

"Deo, we're waiting," says Salie.

The tiger on his neck laughs at me. What did Salie say? Hold on tight and don't let go.

Keelan smiles at me. "I didn't want to tell either, Deo. Please. I want to hear how you came here."

I look at the faces in the circle, all turned toward me. A part of me wants to get up and run out of the room, but another part wants to make my story real for them.

"I once had a brother. His name was Innocent. He was a very special person and he was my best friend."

And so I've begun.

Gutu, and what happened there. Commander Jesus, Amai, and Grandpa Longdrop. Innocent stretched out on the ground covered in ants and piss.

Captain Washington and the visit of the Green Bombas. The song I sang for Innocent.

Short sleeves or long sleeves on the road to Beitbridge. How Innocent saved me from being eaten by the witch. Innocent slipping in the Limpopo River and the water covering his head. Innocent blowing his whistle at the hyena. Innocent packing tomatoes. Innocent disappearing into a hole in a bridge in Jozi. Innocent missing.

The garbage that was not garbage at all.

Innocent dead.

Camp life, without Innocent.

The train ride through the desert to Cape Town, without Innocent. More camp life at the end of the world, without Innocent. Living on the streets, without Innocent, and finding escape in a glue-tube, where everything is out of focus, light and slow. And then, the worst part of it all: how the memory of Innocent blurs, starts to disappear.

"I can no longer remember what my brother looked like. It is as if he has gone forever from my mind and I will never, ever see him again...."

My vision blurs.

I do not know when the tears start rolling down my cheeks, nor do I know when the sob in my chest makes it impossible for me to continue. And the strangest thing of all is that part of me is so sad, it feels like I will never stop crying, and another part is so happy to be talking about Innocent. I have missed my brother so much. He has been away for so long, and now here he is in this room beside me again. I wipe my eyes on the sleeve of my shirt. I can't believe I am crying in front of all these people, and no one is laughing at me.

"I'm finished," I say. "Sorry, it was a bit long."

"But never boring," says T-Jay, and everybody laughs.

Even me.

"Thank you, Deo. Thank you, everyone," says Salie. "You know, as I listened to you, I became more certain than ever that you have the strength to beat any team in the world. Now that you have heard one another's stories, do you understand more about who your teammates are? Don't you think you've all had too much crap in your life to be dishing it out to one another too?"

Salie is right. I'm so tired of fighting; so tired of proving that I do belong. Salie takes the paper out of his pocket.

"There's only one way I can coach this team and there's only one way we are going to win the Street Soccer World Cup.

"We can win only if we play as a team. That means building the strongest damn team spirit in the world! No matter how good a player you are, you will make mistakes, and you will need your fellow players to encourage you and not beat you up!

"I have watched you very closely during the last seven days, and each of you brings something special to this team. Zimbabwe has brought me guts and determination; from Kenya, I get lightness and speed; from Angola, great defense of the goal area; from Mozambique, superb ball control and agility."

Salie stands up and walks around the circle, pinning us back in our seats with eyes as fierce as his tiger tattoo. He prowls behind us, growling with emotion.

"Don't you understand? It is because we are not the same that we are stronger than any other team in this competition! All of you have learned to play soccer in different parts of Africa. Our combined playing style is like no other in the world, and it's difficult to read. I can take the best from where you come from and make you the strongest team in the competition.

"Each person chosen to join this squad will wear South

African colors. But those of you who are not South African will wear a red armband showing the flag of your country. We will show the world that the South African street-soccer side does not ignore our refugees. That we are stronger as a nation because of them!"

Salie stops speaking and stands at the center of the circle, his hands on his hips.

"And if anyone doesn't agree with me or doesn't want to play under these conditions, they can leave this room right now."

Nobody moves. Something shifts inside of me. I never thought I would be able to play for South Africa, but the way Salie explains it, I will be playing for myself, for where I come from, and for my teammates.

Salie nods once and slowly unfolds the piece of paper. "The people taking part in the Street Soccer World Cup tournament will be…"

I hold my breath, like everyone else, waiting to hear what his next words will be.

"…everyone in this room."

Our shouting is deafening. We are on our feet, hugging one another, jumping up and down, chanting, "World Cup here we come, here we come, here we come!"

25

A Midnight Run

It is after midnight and I am wide awake. In ten hours' time, we will be playing our first match of the tournament. Tomorrow, no, today, the Street Soccer World Cup begins. I lie on my bunk bed, my hands behind my head, staring into the darkness. I am dressed in my clothes, waiting for the night to be sleep-still.

The time has come. I imagine I hear the *tap-tapping* on the window, but when I get up to look out the window, I see that the street below is empty. The others have not come back. When I'm sure that everyone is asleep, I pull the small back-pack out from under the bed. I check that it has everything I need, and then, very quietly, I slip out of the room and make my way down the corridor. I start heading down the stairs when a voice from behind stops me.

"Deo, where are you going?"

It's Keelan.

"What are you doing up so late?" I ask. "I thought every-one was asleep."

"I'm too excited to sleep."

"Me too. You want to come for a walk?"

She looks at me, puzzled, but then shrugs. "You know what Salie said, lights out at ten o'clock."

"My light was out at ten o'clock," I say, grinning.

"Let me get my shoes."

In a moment we are both at the front door. I hesitate before turning the handle. "You sure you want to come? I don't want to make any trouble, but I've got to do something, and it's got to be done tonight."

She holds my gaze, then smiles. "Let's go."

The night air falls softly on my skin. The smell of the Lies-beek River is never far away in this part of town, but tonight the air is rich with the taste of sea salt. We walk quickly down the pavement, and I am happy to have Keelan beside me. I start jogging. It feels good to run in the night. Keelan falls in beside me, and our steps become one.

"I won't ask where we're going," she says after a while, "but I am curious. Why are we running through Salt River in the middle of the night?"

"It's not far now. See that highway leading into town?"

She comes up short. "Deo, why there?"

"Relax. It's not what you think. Come on, it will be all right."

The shadows darken as I run away from the street onto a

narrow pathway leading directly under the highway. I pull out my flashlight from my backpack to check that the others are not camping here for the night. The beam of light doesn't fall on any surprised faces or shapes of people sleeping under cardboard. It's a warm evening; they're probably hanging out around Grand Parade. I count the pillars under the highway, looking for one in particular, checking the graffiti with my flashlight. Finally the beam finds the word *KEWL* painted in red. I slip off my backpack and take out the small shovel I borrowed from the YMCA gardener's shed.

"This won't take long," I say. Kneeling down at the base of the pillar, I start digging.

"Deo, have you gone absolutely crazy?" asks Keelan, looking around anxiously.

I don't answer her. I've come for what I buried here a long time ago, when I had nowhere to go and my life was slipping out from underneath me: my billion-dollar soccer ball and Innocent's Bix-box. I pull the ball out of the sand and dust it off.

When I first came to the city, I quickly learned that having something that others didn't wasn't wise. I had to be like the others and own nothing. For a while I was in danger of losing the most precious thing to me. I wasn't ready for the responsibility of looking after Innocent's Bix-box, so I buried it under the highway.

"Okay, let's go," I say, slipping my old cowhide pouch and Innocent's Bix-box into my backpack.

We jog back toward the YMCA. As we turn the corner, I slow down to walk the last three hundred feet.

"Did that belong to your brother?" asks Keelan.

"The box did. He called it his Bix-box."

We go into the deserted dining room and sit down at one of the tables. I pull out my old soccer ball.

"This is mine. It was my first soccer ball. My grandfather made it out of old cowhides, and I used to stuff it with plastic."

Keelan touches the hide, tries to puff the leather out. "I've played with balls a lot worse than this," she says.

I put the Bix-box on the table. I thought it would be difficult to open, but it's not. I open the lid and take out the contents, laying the items one by one on the table: a pocketknife, a whistle, two batteries, a photograph, a piece of soap, a condom, a two-for-the-price-of-one voucher for underarm deodorant, earplugs, and a pocket-size Bible.

"This is the whistle he used to chase away the hyena," I say, lifting up the whistle and remembering my brother running through the bush blowing as loudly as he could.

I touch the pocketknife. "And we used this to cut Patson's crutch off the bamboo when we crossed the Limpopo River."

"Perhaps your brother knew more about sex than you think," says Keelan, picking up the condom.

"Innocent didn't like girls much. He saw safe-sex ads everywhere, and he thought that condoms would keep him safe from girls," I say.

Keelan laughs. "Very sensible," she says, flicking through the pages of the small Bible. "Who's Samuel?"

Her question surprises me.

She reads: "'To Innocent and Deo, This is not a book of laws but a book of love. It will always be your salvation. Love, Samuel.'"

"Let me look at that." I take the Bible from her and read the message on the front page. *To Innocent and Deo*. It's my name.

"What is it, Deo?"

"It's from my father. He wrote something to me. I've never seen this before."

My father is real. I stare down at my name, written by his hand. He knew I existed. I look at the stuff that was so important to Innocent and realize that other than the Bible, most of it is junk. It may have meant something to my brother, but it means nothing to me.

"What?" asks Keelan.

"My old life doesn't exist anymore," I say. "Everything in this box was Innocent's whole life. He couldn't live without his Bix-box." I gather all of Innocent's belongings together. "It was his life. Not mine." I put his treasures back into his Bix-box and close the lid.

"But this is yours," Keelan says, pushing my old leather pouch toward me. "This is what brought you here."

26

MATCH WEEK

We take to the streets of Cape Town, and for one sunny, blue-sky morning, the city belongs to soccer players. Hundreds of people line the streets and cheer as we walk past, waving our flags and making as much noise as we can. I walk down the middle of Adderley Street waving at strangers, laughing at their smiles, loving the noise and excitement. All around me people are singing songs I have never heard before.

"For God and for country! For God and for country! Philippines score! Score! Score!" chants the team behind us as we march on toward the parking lot in front of the newly built Green Point Stadium.

"USA! USA! USA!" chant the players from America.

"Olé, olé, olé, olé, olé," sing the Spaniards.

The team from Ivory Coast beats out a rhythm on their drums. The players from England wave clackers in the air that make an awful racket. The Koreans clap their hands and shake bells. The Austrians blow horns.

The parade finally arrives at Green Point. The soccer stadium towers above the parking lot, where scaffolding stands have been erected around three soccer courts. We gather in front of a stage, where a man waves, greeting the thousands of people in front of him.

"Is that Nelson Mandela?" I ask T-Jay, pointing at the small man with glasses on the stage.

He laughs. "No, that's Bishop Desmond Tutu."

Desmond Tutu raises his hands in the air, and the crowd goes quiet. "There are one billion homeless people in our world today," he says. "And today in South Africa, on this glorious morning, you represent them all. The Street Soccer World Cup exists to end this problem, so that you can all have a home. All year round you are excluded from society, but now is your chance to take center stage. I congratulate you on your gift that has brought you to this World Cup. I thank God for your talent, for your perseverance, and for your courage. This tournament uses soccer to inspire and empower people to change their own lives. You have done that by being here!"

The crowd roars back at him. The sound of horns, clackers, bells, and drums is deafening.

"You are all winners! God bless you all!" shouts Desmond Tutu. "Let the games begin!"

*　　*　　*

There are three minutes left to play in our first match. We are one goal down. The crowd is on its feet. They have not stopped screaming, waving flags, and singing the entire match. The electronic clock is ticking down. Each wasted second brings us closer to our first loss in the tournament. The Danish goalkeeper shouts at his teammates, bouncing the ball in front of him. I have no idea what he is saying; it sounds like he's ordering oodles of noodles!

Two minutes and thirty seconds to go.

The referee blows his whistle, signaling a free kick. "Time wasting!"

Jacko runs up and grabs the ball.

"Quick, Jacko!" I shout. "Over here!"

The seating around the main court is packed with more than five thousand spectators. I try to keep them out of my vision. None of us can get used to the noise or to the intensity of a fast-paced, fourteen-minute game against a team of men all over twenty years old. If not for the frying-pan hands of Godfast, we could be as many as six goals down.

Two minutes to the end.

Jacko flicks the ball against the sidewall. The ball lands neatly at my feet. Ernesto is running down my right side, waiting for the pass. In another second, the Danish defender will be swooping down on me. I keep my head down, feint a pass to Ernesto, and slip past the defender. I run down the center of the court, Jacko screaming on my left, Ernesto screaming on my right. I glance up at the goalkeeper. He crouches low, his arms spread out. There is time for only one more shot at the goal.

I swing my right leg back and drive through the shot, sending the ball to the top right-hand corner. The goalkeeper springs to his right to block my shot. He makes a great save. We will lose our first game.

But he doesn't catch the ball cleanly; it falls to the ground. He has dropped it!

I pounce on the loose ball and toe it between his legs into the net.

Goal!

The crowd goes wild. Jacko, Ernesto, and Godfast jump all over me. The referee blows his whistle. The electronic clock shows that there are still thirty seconds left to play.

"Not yet!" I scream, pushing Jacko off me. "We can still lose."

I see Salie and Tom yelling for us to get back into position. Salie is not as excited as everyone else. The other players on the bench are all on their feet, yelling for us to play on. Salie knows the danger of celebrating too soon. In this game, a lot can happen in thirty seconds.

The Danish players are shouting at the referee for a time-wasting penalty, but we quickly run back to our positions before he can blow us up.

The game restarts. The Danish players come at us like a pack of wild dogs. I tackle, defend, and block every pass or shot that is made at the goal. It is the longest thirty seconds in my life, and then the horn blows and the game is over.

Our first game is a draw.

Salie comes running onto the court. "Okay, we've got one minute to get ready for the penalty shoot-out. There are five shots at goal. Deo, you take the first and the last."

I had forgotten. In street-soccer rules, there can be no draw. There has to be a winner.

"Good luck, Godfast," says Salie as the court is cleared.

The penalty shoot-out begins. I take the first shot. It's not a good strike, and the goalie saves it easily. But Godfast saves the Danish shot. Jacko lines up, kicks, and scores, but then the Danish player gets one past Godfast.

1-1.

Ernesto's turn. He shoots and scores. Godfast saves his next shot, and we go 2-1, one goal up!

Godfast comes forward to take his shot. He powers one straight into the hands of the goalie, who grins at him and trots up to the penalty spot to take his shot at Godfast. God-fast saves it easily and grins back at the Danish goalie.

Now it's my turn again. I must score. I place the ball on the spot, take two steps back, feint left, and power the ball into the right corner. I am able to trick the goalie into moving the wrong way.

It's a goal!

The whole team pours onto the court and piles on top of me. It's our first win!

On the first day of the tournament, we play five matches in the pool stages against teams from Denmark, Spain, Canada, Australia, and Egypt. We lose two and win three. Salie is not happy.

"It looked like you guys were overwhelmed. I've never seen you so sluggish. Keelan, you were running around like you had cement blocks for feet. T-Jay, what happened to your sharp passing? Alfabeto, have you forgotten the patterns we've been working out for the last three weeks? People, you've got to forget the crowd, the noise, the hype—focus on one another and block out everything else."

We sit in the conference room on the morning of the second day. Now I know why stretch exercises are so important. We were up at six this morning, warming up and stretching. I feel like a truck has rolled over me. Tom bandages Ernesto's knee and shakes his head.

"I'm not sure if this is going to heal by tomorrow," he says to Salie. "You may have to rest him for a day."

Salie scowls at him. "Hey, don't shoot the messenger," Tom says. "I wasn't the one who threw him at the Egyptian!"

"People, you have to learn to pace yourselves. Ernesto, you played well and showed real courage, but now you're injured and useless to your team. I need every one of you fit and healthy for the *whole* week," he says. "Remember, there are forty-eight teams with one goal: to go home with one of the six trophies. If we are going to be one of those teams, we need to do a lot better today."

So we do.

By the end of the day, we have won four out of our five matches, beating teams from Belgium, Argentina, Malawi, and Greece. But in our last match of the day, Brazil beats us bad: 5-1.

In our debriefing session the next morning, Salie takes a different approach.

"Losing to world champions is not a disgrace. They had a few lucky goals," he says as we all groan. "No, I mean it. We can beat them, and you're going to get another chance at playing them if we make it through to the group stage. Now, let's sort out our combinations for the rest of the day."

On the third day, T-Jay and I are interviewed by a television station called CNN. The reporter tells us that we are the two highest goal-scorers in the tournament so far. I'm a little nervous as the assistant feeds a cable through the inside of my shirt and clips a small microphone to my collar.

"Look straight at me," says the reporter. "And don't worry about the camera."

I nod and wait for him to finish his introduction. I can't be sure, but I think he's wearing a wig!

"This is so cool," whispers T-Jay as he rubs his finger across his teeth to polish them. "How do I look?"

"Shut up, T-Jay, you look fine," I whisper back as the cameraman looks up and frowns at us. I can't stop staring at the reporter's hair. It's too blond to be real.

"Quiet, please," the cameraman says as he films the reporter.

"This year's Street Soccer World Cup final is taking place in the shadow of the brand-new Green Point Stadium in Cape Town, South Africa. You could call this tournament a mini–dress rehearsal for the FIFA World Cup that kicks off in South Africa in just over three weeks. A lot has been said about how other African teams feel about playing in South Africa, particularly after the xenophobic attacks of just a few years ago. Well, they could learn a lot from the players in this tournament. This unique event draws the homeless off the streets from around the world and brings them together for a week of action-packed soccer.

"People who have been spat at the week before are cheered by thousands. But the South African team has made a bold statement with its unusual inclusion policy.

"In the South African team of twelve players, five are refugees," he says, and the camera moves away from the reporter to focus on T-Jay and me.

"Their coach, Solomon Davids, has instructed each player not born in South Africa to wear a red armband with the flag of the country of the player's birth. This inclusion of refugees in a national team is a remarkable statement and one that has received both praise and criticism. But no one is complaining about the fact that the South African team has just beaten one of the tournament favorites, Germany, four to two. They stand a very good chance of winning the Street Soccer World Cup trophy for the first time.

"With me now are Deo Nyandoro from Zimbabwe and Thomas Jansen from South Africa. They each scored two goals against Germany and effectively shut out a highly organized and disciplined German team.

"Thomas, if I could start with you? How do the other South Africans on the team feel about playing with refugees from other—"

"They're not refugees. They're people," says T-Jay, cutting off the journalist. "I'm sick of all these stupid labels—refugees, asylum seekers, homeless, black, white, colored, pink! Let's get one thing straight: On our team we don't care about labels, we care about good soccer players."

"Um, thank you, Mr. Jansen…"

"The people who come from other African countries to South Africa have been chased out of the townships. Many of them are living on our streets. This is a Street Soccer World Cup. Why shouldn't they play on our team? They are our brothers and sisters, and our country is made stronger because of them."

"Thank you, Mr. Jansen…"

"Call me T-Jay."

"Thank you, Mr. T-Jay. And Deo, how do you feel about playing for South Africa, especially in the light of the xenophobic attacks in Khayelitsha against Somalis and Zimbabweans?"

"I'm here to play soccer. I'm on the team because my coach believes that we can win this tournament. I've been given a chance to show what I can do, and I'm grateful for that," I say, looking straight into the reporter's eyes and trying not to look at his hair or pay any attention to the black lens of the camera.

"And how do you see your future in this country, Deo?"

"In five years' time, I want to be playing in the World Cup final."

"As a South African?"

"As who ever wants me."

The tournament passes in a blur. During the course of the day there is no time to think. Only at night, when everyone is asleep, do I have a chance to think about everything.

I lie in bed, the pocket Bible on my chest, staring up into the darkness, trying to organize my thoughts. I feel a change in me. I see it in the eyes of the rest of the team too. I feel I belong here, not because I've scored goals but because my father wrote my name. It's difficult to explain, but all I know is that the Deo on the run, the Deo of the camps, and the Deo of the streets is gone forever.

On the way back from Green Point this evening, I noticed a big truck with the sign REMOVALS along its side. I watched it as it turned off toward Goodwood, and I thought about asking Salie if we could follow it. I checked its number plate, but it wasn't the same number that Innocent taught me. I have stopped thinking about trying to find my father. I'll give him a chance to try to find me instead.

Keelan amazed me today too. She scored her third goal and headed straight to me. I was sitting on the bench when she threw her arms around me and kissed me on the cheek. It felt good—that she could do that so easily. For the rest of the game I couldn't think of anything else. And I'm still thinking about it now.

There are two more days left of the tournament, and then it will be over. That thought leaves a hole in my stomach. What will I do next week? We have to move out of the YMCA on Sunday night and into a halfway house that the sponsors have organized. There is talk of getting a tutor to prepare us to go back to school. I heard Salie and Tom talking about finding work for some of the older players.

We play four matches tomorrow, and the toughest one will be against the Russians. They have stormed through the group stages, winning most of their games, becoming Cup favorites. Salie believes we stand a good chance of making the finals, but the Russians stand in our path.

After five minutes, we are down 2-0 to the Russians. Nothing has gone according to plan. They are too powerful for us and knock us down like flies.

"What do they put in the water in Russia?" says T-Jay, panting. "Vodka?"

If they score again, we can kiss the final good-bye. We can never come back from three down. The mood in the crowd has changed; they see that we are beaten. Even Godfast has stopped yelling at us from the goal area. We are never able to get the ball, and without possession, we can't score.

Ernesto loses the ball again, and the Russian striker powers down the center of the court and takes aim at the goal. He shoots, and miraculously, Godfast throws himself in the air and manages to get his fingers to the ball, which soars over the boards into the crowd. Godfast lands hard. Salie calls a time-out as Godfast struggles to get back to his feet. Tom and Salie race onto the court, and we gather around Godfast.

While Tom patches up Godfast's elbow, Salie shouts above the noise of the crowd, "They've managed to break you as individuals. Now start playing as a team. Remember where you come from. Use one another!"

The game restarts. We have the ball, finally, but the Russian goal area seems like the other end of the world. T-Jay slips past the first Russian defender and bounces the ball off the boards to Ernesto who, seeing me switch positions to right wing, back heels the ball to me in a smooth move that gets the crowd cheering again.

Without thinking, I do the move Aziz taught me all those years ago at Beitbridge. It comes so naturally that it leaves the Russian striker standing still. I have a free shot at the goal and only seconds to take it, but out of the corner of my eye I see T-Jay running to my left. Without hesitation I pass the ball to him, and he drives the ball past the goalie into the back of the net.

The crowd erupts. Their cheers drown out our on-court celebrations and the halftime horn.

"You see, you can do it!" shouts Salie as we splash our faces with water. "Now I need two more goals exactly like that."

As we enter the court for the second half, the cheer we get is overwhelming. I see a new determination in T-Jay's eyes.

"Vladimir is not going to knock me down in this half," he says, immediately winning the ball from the Russian defender, who makes the mistake of grabbing T-Jay's shirt and pulling him down.

The referee's whistle blasts.

Penalty.

The Russians surround the referee, but he simply points to the spot. Ernesto throws the ball to me.

"You've got the best right foot, Deo. Don't miss," he says.

"No, Ernesto, I think the goalie knows my right foot too well. You take the shot. He won't expect that."

Ernesto places the ball on the spot, and we hold our breath as he steps up and shoots. I hope that I've made the right decision.

Goal!

Ernesto scores and the game is 2-2.

The next five minutes are a furious battle of defense and attack. Nobody wants to go to the lottery of a penalty shoot-out, and the Russians become more desperate with each assault on our goal. Godfast is the hero of the moment as he saves shot after shot, leaving the Russians frustrated and angry.

I no longer hear the noise of the crowd. I have slipped away into a zone of memory and feeling. I am all I ever want to be. I am free of worry, unable to think of anything but this moment. The ball lands at my feet, inviting me to move it up into the Russian goal. In a flash of clarity it all comes back: the games I played in Gutu, Beitbridge, and Khomele village were all in preparation for this moment.

Better make some Deo magic.

I move past one player, bounce the ball off the boards into the air and onto my head, and then I leap off the ground and swivel my right foot to connect with the ball. The shot is perfect, and from fifteen paces away it flies straight past the goalie into the back of the net, taking everyone by surprise.

I land hard on the cement.

The last minute is a blur of defense and wild kicks, and then the horn blasts and the people in the stadium roar.

It's 3-2. South Africa has beaten the Russians. We've made it into the finals!

27

THE FINAL

Ladies and gentlemen, will you please welcome the two teams that have made it to the Street Soccer World Cup final!"

All around me, cheering erupts. We walk out onto the court to face the packed stands. The Brazilian team walks next to us. We line up in the middle of the court and wait for the national anthems to be played. It's the last game of the tournament. Salie said that we could be world-beaters, and he was right.

"I know some of you can't believe you are here," Salie said to us before this game. "Believe it. Now all you have to do is believe that you can be world champions. I believe you can be. But do you?"

The Brazilian national anthem starts to play. I stand with my hand, not on my heart, but on my armband. I am excited but calm. I am bruised and battered all over, but I feel no pain. After playing twenty-two games over six days, I've learned a lot about how to control my emotions, how to shut out pain, how to concentrate. I scan the crowd before me, looking up at row after row of faces. In their eyes I see admiration and respect. These people, who normally would look at me with pity or contempt, see me now in a new way. The South African national anthem starts to play, and the sound of thousands of people singing fills the air.

I imagine I see Amai and Grandpa Longdrop in the crowd, watching and waving at me. There is a smile on my mother's face. I remember it so well. And farther up on the stand, I see the worried face of Captain Washington. He lifts his hands up at me and applauds. One by one, the faces of the people I met on my journey return. I imagine them all looking down on this court and watching me play: Patson and his father; Aziz and Sinbaba at Beitbridge; old Benjamin and his nephew, Philani; my family in the bridge, Catarina, Rais, Angel, Gawalia and his two sons, Rasta and Tsepo; the children from Gutu — Bhuku, Shadrack, Javu, Pelo the Buster, and Lola. Standing right at the back of the stands, I see the huge figure of Mai Maria. She laughs at me, her dreadlocks swirling like snakes. Lennox is there too, clapping.

I realize I am looking for someone else, someone more important than all of these people.

Innocent.

I look carefully from face to face for my brother. I want so bad to see him once more, his radio pressed close to his ear, waving at me, shouting my name. "I need some more batteries, Deo," my brother said to me on the day that I lost him. The memory makes me smile. Innocent might not be in the crowd, but he is in my heart.

The anthems are over. We jog into our positions. The referee holds the ball up and checks that both teams are ready.

I call Keelan, T-Jay, Godfast, and Jacko to the center of the court. We stand close together, our shoulders touching.

"Now is the time to show them what we are and where we come from," I shout. "We will win this game."

I offer my hand. One by one they offer theirs. Our grip is strong, united in purpose.

"Let's play!" we shout.

The crowd roars for the referee to throw the ball into the court. We begin the game.

How it will end, none of us can know. It does not matter. Together, we play the game of our lives.

Author's Note

A photograph of a man burning to death during the xenophobic attacks in South Africa in 2008 forced me to ask the question: If people knew who that burning man was and how he came to be in South Africa, would they have killed him? To better answer that question I decided that I had to find out more about refugees and how they came to be in my country.

While working in the soup kitchen at the Scalabrini Centre of Cape Town (www.scalabrini.org.za) I met three remarkable young Zimbabwean men, Usher Vundhla, Fantam, and Rasta. I spent several hours interviewing them for this novel and in the process discovered that, aside from their refugee status, the one thing they had in common was that none of their fathers was alive: One was killed by the Ghuma-ghuma, one was shot by the soldiers of Mugabe, and one died from HIV/AIDS. The young men, none of them more than twenty years old, were desperate to bring their families to South Africa, but given their lack of resources and the current political climate, this remains a remote possibility. Unfortunately, Usher, Fantam, and Rasta now live on the streets of Cape Town, under highways, and wherever they can find shelter. They refuse to live in the refugee camps set up by the provincial government of the Western Cape. The stories they told me of their journey to Cape Town, while we prepared food for other refugees, inspired much of this novel.

XENOPHOBIA

My description of the xenophobic attacks by the residents of the Alexandra township in the novel is a pale version of what actually happened in South Africa in May 2008. I wanted to imagine what it must be like for two brothers to successfully make it to Johannesburg after a dangerous journey, only to face the hatred of the local people upon arrival. Unfortunately, the burning of Innocent was not something I made up, but was based on an actual event that took place in Alexandra in 2008.

An investigation by the Southern African Migration Project found that high levels of intolerance and hostility toward foreigners by South Africans were the main reason for the wave of xenophobic violence that took place in May 2008. More than sixty people, many of them migrants, were killed during attacks on foreigners throughout the country. More than a thousand suspects were arrested.

The assaults on foreign communities left tens of thousands of migrants without homes following the destruction of their property. The report said the attacks were initially attributed to South Africa's alienating apartheid past, the daily struggle for existence, and the government's failure to redistribute to the poor the fruits of the post-apartheid economic boom.

The study found that 76 percent of those surveyed want the country's borders electrified, while 67 percent want all refugees kept in border camps. For half of those surveyed, enclosing outsiders wasn't enough; they preferred a policy of deportation. The report suggests that South Africans continue to consider foreign nationals a threat to the social and economic well-being of their country. Two-thirds argued that migrants were associated with crime and used up scarce resources, while just under a half felt outsiders brought disease. The report concludes: "The tragic events of May 2008 should act as a major wake-up call to all South Africans. They cannot rest on their laurels. All past and future perpetrators of xenophobic violence should be vigorously prosecuted. What is urgently required is action, not only to ensure that the disgrace is not repeated, but so that South Africans can hold up their heads as they prepare to host a distinctly uneasy world in the 2010 World Cup Soccer final."

Unfortunately, the murderers of "the burning man," as he is now known in South Africa, remain free, and there is very little likelihood of them ever being brought to justice.

(http://en.wikipedia.org/wiki/Xenophobia_in_South_Africa)

THE HOMELESS WORLD CUP

The Homeless World Cup is a life-changing international soccer tournament. From Argentina to Australia, South Africa to Portugal, Cameroon to Brazil, Germany to England, homeless people take a once-in-a-lifetime opportunity to represent their country and change their lives forever. Seventy-seven percent of players go on to find a home, to come off drugs and alcohol, to get into schools, to find jobs, to get training, and to repair relationships with friends and family. This is the future we hope for Deo.

Following the huge success of the first few Homeless World Cup tournaments, the games are now recognized as an annual event on the global sporting calendar.

(www.homelessworldcup.org)

GLOSSARY

amai	Shona word for "mother"
cassava	Large thick root; tastes like a potato when cooked
Chipangano	Youth brigade of Zimbabwean political party
dhoti	Wraparound linen cloth worn by men
Ghuma-ghuma	Criminal gang that preys on refugees
Jozi	Slang word for city of Johannesburg
kak	Slang Afrikaans word used to mean "nonsense"
kraal	Circular African homestead
kwerekwere	Derogatory term for foreigner; word is imitation of how different African languages sound to the local ear
madala	Old man, elder
MDC	Movement for Democratic Change, an opposing Zimbabwean political party
pungwe	Mandatory rally held for propaganda purposes
sadza	Mush made from meal produced by grinding corn
shambok	Animal-hide whip used to herd cattle
spaza	Small general or convenience store in South African townships
wena	Slang African word for "man" or "guy"
Zed	Abbreviation for ZANU PF, Zimbabwean political party

Acknowledgments

I am deeply grateful to all those people who made this book possible:

To the three young men I met at Scalabrini—Usher Vundhla, Fantam, and Rasta—thank you for telling me your story; Amy Kaplan for her insight and "no editing" approach to criticism; Ellen-Anne and Emma, my two lovely daughters, for their patience with Dad's constant refrain, "I've got to work tonight, girls"; and my dearest wife, Ettie, for her editing skill and wonderful, loving support.

"Diamonds for everyone."

That's what fifteen-year-old Patson Moyo hears when his family arrives in the Marange diamond fields. Soon Patson is working in the mines himself, hoping to find his *girazi*—the priceless stone that could change his life forever. But when the government's soldiers come to Marange, Patson's world is shattered.

Don't miss Michael Williams's *Diamond Boy*, a high-stakes, harrowing adventure in the blood-diamond fields of southern Africa. A companion novel to *Now Is the Time for Running*.

Available December 2014 however books are sold